Louis Jacolliot, Warren Franklin Kellogg

# Hunting in the Jungle with Gun and Guide After Large Game

Louis Jacolliot, Warren Franklin Kellogg

**Hunting in the Jungle with Gun and Guide After Large Game**

ISBN/EAN: 9783337045791

Printed in Europe, USA, Canada, Australia, Japan

Cover: Foto ©Andreas Hilbeck / pixelio.de

More available books at **www.hansebooks.com**

HE CAME WITH HEAD UP, A SUPERB SIGHT.

# HUNTING IN THE JUNGLE

## WITH GUN AND GUIDE

### *AFTER LARGE GAME*

ADAPTED FROM "LES ANIMAUX SAUVAGES" BY

WARREN F. KELLOGG

ILLUSTRATED

BOSTON

ESTES AND LAURIAT

PUBLISHERS

# CONTENTS.

# LIST OF ILLUSTRATIONS.

# HUNTING IN THE JUNGLE

## WITH GUN AND GUIDE.

---

### CHAPTER I.

#### OFF FOR THE JUNGLE.

WAS young and fond of adventure, full of spirits and good health; and when my friend the Captain offered me a bunk in his own cabin for an African voyage, I promptly gave up my desk and duties in a New York shipping-house, and accepted the invitation at once. It was a long voyage, but its tedium was relieved for me by an occasional shot at some bird lost in the desert of waters, or by the capture of an unwary shark or porpoise when a long calm gave the men the leisure to think of such sport. Then in the watches of the summer nights the Captain and I would pace the deck for hours, while he spun me yarns of shipwreck and adventure on every coast. He had been in the English service, on this very African station. when the energies of the Royal

Navy were exerted against the slave-trade. His reminiscences of this revolting business furnished matter for many exciting stories, of which "A Night on an African Cruiser" is a fair example.

"We were cruising off the mouth of the Congo, looking out for slavers, and as a pleasant change, in the middle of the rainy season. the night was starlight. The cheering cry of 'Sail ho!' aroused the slumbering watch of H. M. Brig 'Pantaloon.' of which I was first officer, and dispelled my half-waking dreams. Sending word to the captain, I made all sail on the ship. and in a few minutes our spars were covered with canvas and the brig gliding through the smooth water before the land-wind which had just sprung up.

"Our men clustered forward eagerly trying to discover the chase, which as yet was visible to no eyes except those of the Krooman at the masthead who had first reported the strange sail. As a colored man's power of vision is generally superior at night to that of a white man, the suspense was endured for nearly a quarter of an hour, when the good faith of the lookout was verified, the strange sail being plainly visible from deck on the line of the horizon, and the distance between the 'Pantaloon' and her prey rapidly lessening.

"'Clear away the gun forward, and give her a blank cartridge!' was an order obeyed as soon as given. The long thirty-two pounder bellowed forth, and the flash lit up for a moment the excited faces grouped around.

As the report died away, all eyes were bent on the chase to see if she obeyed that authoritative signal to 'heave to;' but her white sails still gleamed in the moonlight, and she pursued her course regardless of the mandate. This perseverance in attempting to escape gave good assurance that we were in pursuit of a slave-ship. Many of the crew began already in imagination to spend their prize-money; the Kroomen especially were chuckling with delight, for the very day before, at their earnest request, the figure-head of the 'Pantaloon' had had his spectacles repainted ' to make him see better.'

"The proverbial 'slip 'twixt the cup and the lip' had, however, yet to be illustrated. The guns had been reloaded. this time with shot, and the gunner was standing lanyard in hand awaiting the order to fire, when the captain's attention was attracted by the flapping of the sails — hitherto drawing full — against the masts. The land-wind had suddenly subsided, and a hot stifling calm succeeded. On looking round we discovered in one quarter of the horizon the small cloud, literally ' like a man's hand,' which to experienced eyes betokens the quick approach of a tornado. If one of these awful tropical storms should strike the ship while all sail was set, nothing but the loss of her masts could save her.

" No time now to think of anything but the safety of the ship. 'Hands shorten sail! Quick, men ! quick, for your lives !' shouted the captain. The crew, aware of the danger. worked well. Sail after sail was taken in.

until, instead of a cloud of canvas, the cruiser showed nothing aloft but the clear tracery of spars and rigging. In time, and only just in time, was the work finished, the ship made snug, and the men down from aloft.

"Meanwhile the cloud had rapidly increased in volume until it overspread half the horizon, the remainder of the heavens being still bright and clear. The dead silence of expectation was broken by a low growl of thunder. One breath of wind, cold as from an ice-cave, passed over us; a few big drops of rain splashed upon the deck: then, with a mighty roar, lashing the water into foam, the tornado swept down upon us.

"Notwithstanding all our precautions, the first shock threw the 'Pantaloon' nearly on her beam-ends. For a full minute of painful suspense she remained in that position, then, suddenly righting, — all her timbers groaning, — she yielded to her helm and sped before the hurricane.

"Immediate danger was now over, it being only necessary to keep the ship before the wind until the storm had passed over us. The officers, released from their deepest anxiety, were able to note — some even to enjoy — the magnificent spectacle of an African tornado. In that roaring wind and deafening thunder no man could hear his fellow speak, nor in the darkness see the rope to which he clung or the deck on which he stood, save when the blinding lightning at quick-recurring intervals disclosed the wild scene around him.

THE BLINDING LIGHTNING AT QUICK-RECURRING INTERVALS DISCLOSED
THE WILD SCENE AROUND.

"Two hours passed thus, and the fury of the gale began to abate, when with a simultaneous crash of thunder the lightning struck our foremast. On reaching the deck, the electric fluid was first attracted by the chain cable, along which it ran hissing, until reaching the quarter-deck it leaped with a loud report to the nearest gun, flashing from gun to gun until it plunged into the sea astern, — the old helmsman, as it passed, ducking his head as he would to an enemy's shot. Happily no one was seriously hurt, although some men standing around the mast were partially stunned. The thunder now ceased, and the wind fell. Quitting my station on the forecastle I joined the officers on the quarter-deck, where we congratulated ourselves that the elements had done their worst, and speculated on the chances of the morning light gladdening our eyes with a view of the lost slaver. In all probability, however, she had either been capsized or driven far beyond our reach.

"In these southern latitudes no soft dawn intervenes between the blackest night and glaring, broiling day. No sooner did day break than all eyes were anxiously engaged sweeping the horizon in hopes of encountering the lost slaver. Fifty voices quickly exclaimed, 'There she is!' and there, indeed, not two miles off, lay the luckless vessel that even the tornado had failed to save. The sea was calm; not a ripple disturbed its glassy smoothness as it heaved gently in the long, low ground-swell. It was evident to the crew of the slave-ship that no chance of escape remained; although armed they were no match for an English cruiser. Soon a Brazilian ensign fluttered up to her mast-head, waved there a moment, and then slowly and reluctantly descended in token of surrender.

" Our boats, well manned and armed, pulled toward the prize, passing through some dozens of empty wine-bottles recently thrown overboard, showing that the slaver's crew had begun to drown their sorrows in the good liquor the cabin stores afforded, determined it should not be wasted on their captors. Lazily floating close to the vessel, showing too clearly the nature of her cargo, were several large sharks. Attracted by the scent, these monsters of the deep follow in the wake of slave-ships, accompanying them across the Atlantic, and becoming the floating graves of many a victim to the horrors of the voyage.

" On boarding the prize, she proved to be the 'Aventureiro,' a fine yacht-like schooner carrying one long swivel-gun amidships. There was small need to inquire of her sullen commander whether the cargo was lawful or contraband, and our sailors at once proceeded to open the hatches. On removing the close coverings a dense steaming mist of foul air ascended from the slave-deck below; and three hundred unhappy beings of both sexes were discovered lying down, their feet manacled to long iron bars placed fore and aft through the ship. From this piteous, writhing mass of humanity arose strange cries and shouts of joy when their irons were struck off, and the fact of their deliverance began to dawn upon their minds. The crew of the slaver, twenty-four all told, were transferred to the 'Pantaloon,' and a lieutenant and prize crew were detailed to convey the schooner to Sierra Leone. Before parting company, however, an exciting scene of plunder was enacted, officers and sailors keenly searching after comestibles which — although articles of daily food on

THE LOW LINE OF THE AFRICAN SHORE.

shore — were luxuries to men shut up for months in an African cruiser.

"Tins of preserved meats, sardines, potted salmon, and lobster; boxes of sugar, raisins, butter, wine, and ale rewarded the laughing plunderers, and were passed into the ship under the very eyes of the slave-captain. Soon, however, his face cleared up and he puffed his paper cheroot with calmness, consoled, doubtless, by the recollection of former successful trips ; for slave-traders confess that if one vessel out of four escapes they are amply repaid.

" And now, all arrangements being complete, the ' Aventureiro,' with England's flag at the peak, bore away to the westward, while the 'Pantaloon' once more turned toward her cruising ground."

With tales like this my friend the Captain beguiled the voyage, so that I was almost sorry late one bright afternoon to see the low line of the African shore, and later to cast anchor in the harbor of Sierra Leone.

# CHAPTER II.

## I MEET THURSDAY.

 HAD a letter of credit on a trader in the town, and at our first interview told him of my intention of passing five or six months in the interior to complete my natural history collections. He promised to get me a guide on whose faithfulness I might rely. And sure enough, a few days later he sent me a strapping great fellow as black as the ace of spades. He bore the euphonious name of N'Otoone, and agreed, for the modest sum of ten cents per day, to guide me through forest, jungle, and swamp as far, if I liked, as the Mozambique coast line! Life was too short to make use of a name like his; and bearing in mind Robinson Crusoe's admirable example and the day on which N'Otoone was presented to me, I nicknamed him Thursday, — a title in which he learned to feel the greatest pride after I had told him of great Thor's warlike attributes. As Thursday, therefore, he will appear in future in these pages. He talked English a little, and that was a great thing for me, for it would allow me to enjoy the stories he would be sure to tell, — his countrymen being

all natural *raconteurs*. Besides, I much preferred not to be obliged to use the decidedly unsatisfactory language of signs with a man with whom I was to live some months.

" He is everything desirable," my banker said. " I have known him the last ten years, during which he has come to barter ivory and skins with me, and he will not dare, if only on business policy, to play you any very bad trick. He is a liar. a thief, a bully. and a drunkard, like all of them ; but aside from that," with a smile, " you may depend upon him."

The portrait of the illustrious Thursday is a simple matter, for the trader had faithfully outlined his moral nature in his " recommendation." Physically he was a tall. well-built fellow with tightly curling hair, his teeth filed to a point, which gave him a singularly ferocious appearance closely resembling a shark. He was *dressed* in a belt, from which in front hung a leopard's skin, while across his back were slung a single-barrelled gun and a great iron-wood bow over six feet long. Through his belt was stuck an English axe. of which he was very proud, and in the use of which he was extremely clever.

He belonged to the cannibal race of Fans, which for the last fifty years have little by little overrun the west coast of Africa without any one knowing from what part of the interior they come. Thursday pretended he had become quite civilized by his intercourse with the whites, and that he no longer ate human flesh, — leaving that, as he said, " to the poor blacks who," with a superb gesture, "were not in the habit of living among the officers and traders." If his own stories were to be believed he was one of the most skilful elephant hunters in the neighborhood, and, in fact, he had come almost daily to the trading posts to barter ivory tusks.

Around his neck he wore a string of charms — tigers' and alligators' teeth and bits of stags' antlers — to preserve him from fever, accidents, bad luck, and the bite of snakes. He offered me several, urging me especially to accept one that would protect me from evil spirits. At first I laughed at him, but finding this offended him I took his panther's tooth and put it in my pocket, whereupon he seemed satisfied.

His wife, who accompanied him, wore even less, if possible, than himself. She was a gentle, submissive creature, who carried our drinking water and, aided by her son, a good-looking lad of ten or a dozen years of age, prepared our meals.

As you see, our little caravan was lightly loaded and few in numbers, which is, I think, the only way to travel in equatorial Africa, where it is impossible to make two negroes agree for more than a week, unless to rob and abandon you some fine night in the midst of the forest. I was not afraid of this fate myself, although it has happened to so many explorers, for I intended to go inland not further than forty or fifty leagues. At that distance the traders almost always ultimately learn the fate of any missing European, and there are plenty of ways to avenge their murder. The traders' own personal safety demands that the white man's life shall not be at the mercy of every black devil who covets his arms or his blanket.

I had no desire to solve any knotty questions of physical geography. nor to cross the continent from sea to sea. My wishes were much more modest. namely. — to collect specimens of all the varieties of apes in the country, especially of the gorilla, shooting them myself.

The evening of the very day of our departure. when we had pitched our camp in a little negro village, where the chiefs had placed huts at our disposal, I told Thursday my plan of hunting the " man-eater." He seemed a trifle astonished. but casting a glance at my rifle, which carries an explosive ball whose terrible effect he had seen that very afternoon on a hare that I had literally torn to pieces, he replied that nothing was easier, and that he would guide me to their favorite haunts.

The chiefs of the village were seated in a circle around us. and when my guide explained my project to them they all began to jabber and gesticulate at a tremendous rate. At my request. Thursday translated with great volubility a series of adventures with this curious animal so remarkable that only a negro imagination could invent such tales. For instance. they believe that the " man-eater" is not always an animal like other apes. but that he is possessed by the spirit of some native who, for his evil ways, is condemned to return to this world in the

A FAMILY OF GORILLAS.

monster's body before being admitted to the happy hunting grounds. These "haunted" gorillas, besides enormous strength, have intelligence as great as man's. They
can neither be caught nor killed; they are invulnerable,
even the balls from the white man's rifle flattening themselves upon them, — not because their hides are any
tougher than the others, but because they are protected
by a mysterious charm. According to these trustworthy
accounts some poor woman is compelled to act as companion and servant to these fearful brutes. All day long
she grinds the meal, grates the cassava, and prepares the
food for her master. Should she endeavor to escape she
is immediately torn to pieces; and that is the reason, so
these imperturbable liars assert, that not one of them has
ever been seen to come back.

I should never end were I to tell you all the stories I
heard that night, for, spurred on by Thursday, each man
present wished to add his experience with haunted gorillas to the general testimony. I have told enough to show
the character of the people among whom I was. Given
two possible explanations of an occurrence, one simple
and the other of a marvellous nature, the negro will
choose the latter every time, not from a desire to deceive
but simply to gratify his vivid imagination. So you see
a traveller must take their statements, even on subjects
pertaining to their own country, which they ought to
know best, with a very large grain of salt.

In spite of my wish to bring the conversation round to

the habits of the gorilla that I intended to hunt, on this my first night in camp I could not lead the negroes away from the attractive subject of haunted gorillas, and the long evening was filled with tales of them alone. Wearied with my useless efforts, I threw myself on a mat in the chief's hut and was soon fast asleep, lulled by the voices of the natives, who continued their endless stories till after midnight.

ALL DAY LONG SHE GRINDS THE MEAL.

# CHAPTER III.

## MY FIRST GORILLA.

T daybreak Thursday aroused me, and after a cup of black coffee, prepared by his wife, we took up our march through a vast plain, broken here and there by clumps of palms lifting their tall heads amidst fields of maize and corn. Through the foliage we caught glimpses of hazy mountains far away on the horizon. My guide said they were wooded hills, the haunt of gorillas and elephants, where he had always found plenty of game.

Nothing can be more lovely than the African forests early in the morning. We were threading narrow trails, hardly disturbed by the bare feet of the native hunters, between endless hedges of banana and young palm trees covered with their golden and savory fruit; while between their trunks we could see long stretches of green, wavy grass, soft as velvet in the morning light.

Soon the cultivation ceased, and the land for miles was covered with pepper-plant and flowering tulip, filled with brilliant paroquets that flew away with sharp notes at our approach. On all sides of us, and within a space a

few hundred yards square, were all the most singular
tropical varieties of the equatorial flora. If I had followed simply my tastes I should immediately have given

A MONKEY, SOME FOWLS, AND A BUNCH OF BANANAS.

up my plans for hunting and have remained in this bot-
anists' paradise adding to my herbarium. But — I was
equipped with rifles and cartridges, and it was too late to
alter the object of my journey.

We camped that evening in another native village, and the next morning really entered the unbroken forest. It was now necessary to observe the greatest caution, as at any moment we might meet a tiger, a panther, or a gorilla.

However, before night we arrived without adventure of any kind at the Fan village whence Thursday came. The chief, to whom he introduced me, shook hands with me in the European fashion and asked me if I had not a present for him! This was a sure sign that civilization had reached as far as this town, at least. I gave him an old pistol, at which he seemed greatly pleased, and told him I had come to shoot a "man-eater." He promised to go with us the next morning, and then invited me to a feast at which a monkey, some fowls, and a bunch of bananas cooked in the ashes composed the bill of fare. The monkey was not at all to my taste, and I confined myself to the other dainties; but the Fans devoured in an instant all that I left.

We started early, the chief and Thursday leading us up a narrow valley in which, they both agreed, gorillas were sure to be found.

"Have you ever shot a gorilla?" asked the chief, turning to me as we walked along.

"No, never," I replied.

"Then I will give you a bit of advice," said he. "Which gun are you going to use?"

"This" — pointing to my rifle — "is my favorite, for although the other is double-barrelled, this one is much more effective, for it carries an explosive ball. A wound from it is always fatal."

"The white man is helped by the Great Spirit, who shows him new ways of killing."

"I will show you its merits at the first opportunity," I said.

"Every white man has his fetich who aids him to do wonders; but he can do nothing against the 'man-eater' unless the black men help him."

"Quite true," I said; "we could do nothing without you."

The chief, at these words, threw back his head and glanced with pride at his followers, for his vanity was pleased.

"Listen," he said after a moment. "As you have never hunted the gorilla, I will speak words of wisdom to you."

"Believe me. I will give it my best attention, chief."

"It is not difficult to kill a gorilla. One bullet in his breast, and he is dead."

"So I have already heard; but I am very glad to have this confirmation of it from an authority and a great chief."

The old man looked at me with intense satisfaction. With these few words I had made a friend forever.

"But you must not miss him," he continued, "for he will not give you a second chance."

"That's so," said my guide, as he translated this.

"You could not get your second gun from the boy before he would be upon you, and you would be crushed to a jelly."

At that moment the whole line, as if instinctively, came to a halt. The native guide leading us gave a signal as agreed.

"In which direction?" the chief signed.

The guide pointed ahead of us, a little to the right, toward a clump of tall trees.

"Wait for me here," said the chief, with that sharp tone of command which he knew so well how to assume toward his men. Then, turning to me, —

"Let the white captain follow me."

No sooner had my interpreter translated this to me than the chief dropped on all fours and began to crawl in the direction the scout had indicated. I followed suit, feeling that I was on the eve of a new and exciting experience.

For five minutes, that seemed an age, I saw the chief moving slowly without the least noise, parting the underbrush with his hands, and holding it one side until I too had passed. Suddenly he stopped, half raised himself, and seemed to centre all his attention on a point in space beyond the close curtain of foliage in front of us. My heart beat in great throbs. Finally he made me a sign to approach, and I, in turn, cast a rapid glance through the forest. I felt my hair stand on end as, at the end of a little clearing, I saw seated on a leafy hut an enormous gorilla, sniffing the air and rolling his angry eyes in every direction.

It was my first sight of this curious and terrible animal,—the main cause of my journey and explorations. You would have said that he scented the danger, for his eyes searched the leafy screen behind which we were crouching with a singularly ferocious glance that clearly showed he did not for an instant mistake the direction from which his enemy was coming.

The old chief, used as he was to this sight, took it coolly enough; but a profound astonishment, coupled with a certain kind of terror, literally transfixed me to the spot. I did not expect to see an animal of such terrible proportions and ferocity, and it was one of the rarest experiences of my long life of travel and adventure to find the reality far exceed my wildest imagination.

Erect, his head thrust forward, beating his chest with his long arms, he gave three mighty roars, in which that tone peculiar to wild beasts was curiously mingled with a human cry that might have come from one of our own throats. Then he uttered a series of growls, deep and heavy, louder at first, running down the scale, and diminishing in volume like a clap of thunder rolling away in the distance.

Suddenly the shrill note of a paroquet sounded near us. The gorilla stopped short in astonishment. Instinctively I raised my head to see on which branch this daring

AN ENORMOUS GORILLA, ROLLING HIS ANGRY EYES IN EVERY DIRECTION.

bird was perched. I saw nothing; but when the note was repeated, I realized that I had been deceived by an admirable imitation, and that the old chief had used this signal to call his hunters around us again.

However skilful the Fan chief was in cheating me, he evidently had not deceived the gorilla, for his fury redoubled. At this instant the natives joined us, crawling through the dense undergrowth as we had done.

"Chief," said Thursday, in a whisper so low it hardly reached me, " the brute has already detected us."

" How do you know that ?" said I, softly.

" Look !" he replied; " his nostrils quiver with anger as he scents us, and his cruel eye never leaves our shelter."

" Then why does he not attack us ?  Is he afraid ?"

" Fear !  The man-eater ?  You'll not believe that long."

" Why does he wait, either to run or fight ?"  As I whispered these words the old chief made me a sign, urging me to silence.  The furious cries and roars of the gorilla grew louder and fiercer.  It was plain, even to so inexperienced a hunter as myself, that something unusual was about to happen.  The monster gnashed his tremendous teeth, shaking with rage, but did not leave his hut-roof.  For the twentieth time I asked myself the double question, " Why do we not give him a shot, or why does he not get away from us?"  A dozen times I raised my rifle, — the one carrying the explosive ball. —

and a dozen times the chief threw up the barrel.  I did
not have to wait long for a solution of the mystery.   As
I was watching our enemy with the closest attention.

SHE SPRANG FROM HER SHELTER HOLDING A LITTLE GORILLA.

fascinated by the strange sight. Thursday made me a
sign to look lower.  I obeyed mechanically, and saw, with
a shudder of horror. a second gorilla's head emerging
from the foliage which shaded the hut.

"That is the female," said Thursday. "Now you see why the gorilla did not attack us. He is in a tremendous rage because, in spite of his repeated calls, he cannot make his companion listen."

"What does he want?"

"He wants to see her safe in the forest, and then he will come and settle his account with us. But she is undoubtedly suckling her young, and does not wish to come from her retreat, especially without knowing exactly which way to turn to put her offspring in safety."

In a few moments she seemed to decide, for with a single bound she sprang from her shelter holding a little gorilla, hardly more than a few days old, in her arms. Evidently the little animal *had* been the cause of her hesitation and delay. Her remarkable intelligence showed her almost instantly on which side the danger lay, and facing round, she sprang into the forest without a cry.

Her departure was saluted by a roar from the male more terrible even than its predecessors. I felt my hair stand on end, as it well might before so remarkable a sight.

At a word from the chief, Thursday said, "Do you want to kill him?"

I made a quick gesture of assent.

"Then," said he, with a glance at the chief, "we must show ourselves at once, or he will escape."

We stepped quickly out into the clearing toward the brute, who stopped on seeing us coming.

"Don't shoot until I give the word," whispered the chief. It was not a time to dispute such a singular command, so I merely waited with my gun ready.

The monster was about fifty paces in front of us, and I could easily have shot him where he stood, but resisted the temptation. Whenever I have hunted in Africa with the native chiefs I have always made it a rule to follow their suggestions implicitly, — with due regard, of course, to my own personal safety. You can be pretty sure that these men, used as they are to the wild beasts in their forests, will not give unnecessary advice; and I have always found it paid in the end.

The gorilla had dropped upon all fours, — the attitude in which he travels most easily, — but sight of us renewed his fury in an instant. He stood erect on his long limbs, and with a roar that shook the forest, advanced slowly, but without hesitation, toward us, beating his breast with his arms. This seemed a favorite gesture with him, for in the ten minutes we had been watching him he had three times made use of it. I cannot better describe the noise accompanying it than to compare it to the native tam-tams, as played in the funeral processions. He struck his chest tremendous blows in a rhythmical way, broken by perfect roulades of roars, and his eyes flashed fire. The chief made me a courteous sign that he gave me the first shot; and Thursday, translating, said: " Wait until he has passed the trunk of that palm; and above all, do not miss him!"

The tree he meant was not more than twenty paces from us. I raised my rifle carefully; the gorilla was approaching us. I aimed full at his breast; he had

I AIMED FULL AT HIS BREAST.

hardly crossed the line when my rifle-shot rang through the forest, and the huge brute fell without a cry.

The report had been deafening. I sprang forward to

see the effect of the explosive ball, but Thursday held me back.

"Look out," he cried; "he may yet have some life in him; and one blow from his talon-like fingers would lay you open like a squirrel."

The advice was too good to be disregarded, though from my experience in shooting with this terrible form of ammunition I felt sure he was dead; for I never have seen an animal live if the ball once reaches him. And indeed this case proved no exception; the gorilla was dead.

When the natives saw the terrible wound which he had received, they looked at my rifle with frightened glances, and began to whisper together.

"What do they say?" I asked Thursday.

"That they would give twelve slaves for such an arm."

Such envy did not please me at all. How many travellers have been killed in Central Africa precisely on account of their too tempting fire-arms! I immediately hit upon a device to protect at once my rifle and myself. I happened to have in my belt a line of empty cartridges to be used for small game, and to be loaded with whatever charge of powder and ball the animal I was after required. I loaded my rifle rather ostentatiously with one of these cartridges, capped only, and handing it to the chief himself, I stepped about a yard from the end of the barrel and asked him to fire at me, aiming at my heart. As he hesitated, I said to him: "Do as I bid, for the rifle cannot harm me; it is a fetich. and only kills in my hands."

I fancy Thursday translated this literally. for the old chief raised the rifle at once and pulled the trigger. There was the faint report of the cap, and that was all. M'Yenga returned the rifle hastily; and he and the other natives, as if fearful lest some of its evil influence should affect them, moved off to a respectful distance. Superstition has such a hold on this people that not one of them would have accepted as a gift the gun that a moment before they all coveted. I was safe on that score.

On measuring the gorilla, we found his waist nearly two yards in circumference, proving him to be one of the largest of his species. I asked Thursday why the chief had not allowed me to shoot the female, leaving the hunters to fire simultaneously upon the male, so that we might take the little one alive and try to bring it up on cow's milk and make our first experiment in domesticating the gorilla. Of course I said nothing to them about the scientific interest in such an experiment, for science was a dead letter to them; but I promised a liberal reward to any one who should bring me a young gorilla alive. They all assured me that that was easy enough, but that without its mother it could not live more than three or four days; that the leopard or tiger could be tamed, but never the gorilla, etc.; but it all seemed hearsay. and not one of the hunters spoke from personal experience. Thursday explained that if I had aimed at and missed the female we should have had two gorillas instead of one to fight, and that there would have certainly been a loss of life; and that he could get me a young gorilla *immediately*. He failed to fulfil this promise, however, for it is not at all easy to get one of these young animals, whom the parents defend fiercely with their lives. Chance, often more to be depended on than the most persistent efforts, brought about my wish, but long after this first hunt, which proved conclusively that this species of gorilla builds a rude hut, and that the male, when it shelters his offspring, sits like a sentinel upon its roof to watch over his young. It also seemed settled beyond a doubt, from what I was told and had myself seen, that the gorilla attacks man without hesitation at sight and without waiting to be wounded, while the female attends entirely to the safety of her young without a thought of fighting.

We camped a whole day here for me to preserve and mount the gorilla's head. The natives divided the flesh among themselves, broiling it over the hot coals and eating it half raw. Try as I would, for I should have been glad to learn the taste of this singular meat, I could not overcome my repugnance to this half-human flesh. The brain was not eaten, but carefully wrapped in banana leaf and sent back to the medicine-men of the village, who make from it, the old chief informed me, a magic ointment of most marvellous virtue to protect from all evil, especially from the evil influence of the man-eater. I

THIS GORILLA BUILDS A RUDE HUT.

looked him square in the face. The old hypocrite never winced, and ended his remarks with a fresh demand for rum, of which I gave him a very modest amount, dividing what was left in my flask between him and Thursday.

The first gorilla had fallen; the chief had fulfilled his promise; and nothing remained but to return to the village and end the chase. I made the chief the presents I had agreed to, adding a little keg of rum for the other natives who had accompanied me. and I stayed with them a week. When I had made up my mind to depart the chiefs collected to bid me farewell; and then came a ceremony which, among the Fans, celebrates the adoption of a stranger by the tribe. The old chief held my arm, and pricking it lightly with a thorn, drew a drop of blood. He then did the same to his own; whereupon another chief took these two drops of blood upon two little reeds and transferred them, his to mine and mine to his arm. "Now." said the chief, "you are their white brother, for you have become my son. Wherever you may travel among the Fan tribes you will be received as one of us." Among all peoples of a rude degree of civilization this queer custom of adoption exists, with different ceremonies but the same general idea; and it appears even later among more civilized races in the gift of the freedom of the city. There is no longer an interchange of blood, but it is still the adoption of a *stranger*. I have already alluded to the fact that, during my stay in the village, although all the hunters endeavored to obtain my offered reward, not one was able to catch a young gorilla for me, and that it was to chance I finally owed the possession of one.

On leaving my Fan friends I had told Thursday of my plan to travel toward the river Rembo, striking it about the spot where, making a sudden turn at right angles, it flows swiftly northward and, fifty or sixty miles away, plunges into the sea. I had been told that this country was full of gorillas and every variety of monkey. As the neighborhood of the coast was unhealthy, because of the large number of marshes there, we turned east and journeyed through higher wooded lands. These forests are the haunts of numerous small game, — deer, hare. and wild fowl, — in such numbers that it precluded the danger of hunger.

Five days after my departure we had struck the light tent that I always used in the woods,— for nothing is more unhealthy than the night dews in the African forests, — and I was walking ahead talking with Thursday ; behind us came his wife and boy, and. behind them, my five porters, humming an air in their nasal tones in time to their step. like sailors who join in a refrain as they stamp round the capstan. Suddenly Thursday stopped, making us a sign to do the same. I was carrying my rifle on my shoulder. but as quick as thought I dropped the barrel into my left hand and stood ready. It does not do ever to be surprised in these woods, and a second's hesitation often costs dear.

"What is it?" said I, quickly.

"Did you not hear that cry?"

"Well?"

"It was that of a young gorilla calling its dam."

"Are you sure?"

"Perfectly. Be ready to shoot. Either the old gorilla is too far away to hear, or she does not suspect our presence. I hear no rustling of the leaves. Come, but be careful." We two had advanced hardly breathing. A second cry, a little ahead of us, pierced the silence of the forest. I was so excited that it seemed as though my heart beat audibly. Thursday still preceded me. Suddenly I heard him pronounce the two words, "Look out!" and I saw him raise his gun quickly and fire. and before I had time to turn round, a shiny black mass covered with blood hurled itself upon my guide. Quick as thought I drew my revolver and blew the gorilla's brains out at the instant when he was about to garrote poor Thursday.

The guide, who was not hurt, with the exception of a few scratches on his shoulder, had sprung up and, with a triumphant shout, seized a little gorilla by the nape of the neck and handed it to me. Imagine my pleasure, for I had almost given up hope of ever getting a really young gorilla alive. I could not resist reproving Thursday. however, telling him that he had run a great risk; for had I not been within five feet of him I could never have made my prompt shot before the gorilla would have twisted his neck for him.  I was so excited that I should have quite forgotten to thank Thursday for having thus in cold blood risked his life to satisfy a wish which to him must have seemed a mere whim, when he recalled me to the situation by saying quietly, —

"The white captain is good ; he will give his slave the reward, as agreed."

"What reward?" cried I, in astonishment.

"Did not the captain promise the Fans that he would give a double-barrelled hunting-gun and a keg of rum to any one of them bringing him a young man-eater?"

"Yes."

"Well, Thursday is a Fan, and has brought you such a prize."

"And you ask me to pay you, therefore —"

"What you promised."

"All right, so be it.  I prefer a business view of it myself.  Here are the gun and proper ammunition. for of course they go together ; but I do not propose to give you all the rum at once."

"The white chief is generous and great, but why not?"

"Because you are in my service, engaged for the entire trip, and I don't propose to have you drunk or your faculties muddled for the next week or so, as you know you would be.  If you like, however, I will give you a glass every day until you have had the whole keg.  If you don't like this plan, I will, instead, give you the

THE GUIDE, WITH A TRIUMPHANT SHOUT, SEIZED THE LITTLE GORILLA BY THE NAPE OF THE NECK.

entire keg when we reach Cape Lopez at the end of the trip."

" I prefer the latter." he decided.

I was afraid for a moment that this might set discontent at work in the African's head. But I was mistaken, quite. The African does nothing for nothing. He has no idea of devotion in putting himself into danger; he simply wishes to get a keg of fire-water upon which to become drunk at his leisure ; and Thursday appreciated my right to his entire energy and wit to guide our little caravan through a country where danger is the rule.

At last I had my young gorilla; and I began at once his education by whipping him gently with a bit of banyan wood. which frightened him so that he left off biting at me immediately !

I could not carry out my experiments while we were on the march, so I decided to camp a few days in the first village we came to, which happened to be Stromby, a rather important town twenty-five or thirty kilometres east of Rembo. The king of the country had already met a number of white traders who had come thither for ivory ; and he received me in a most friendly manner. and announced to his subjects assembled that I was " his brother" and was to be respected as such. This done. he gave me his hand, which is a sign not to be misunderstood, as it stands for the same thing in every country of whatever degree of civilization under the sun.

I presented him with a revolver and a music-box, and although he was pleased with the former, the latter delighted his soul. Tying it round his neck he went up and down through the village turning the crank and followed by a wondering crowd of his subjects of both sexes, uttering cries of astonishment and pleasure. Having thus assured my position and treatment in the village I could turn my attention to attempts at civilizing my ugly pet.

# CHAPTER IV.

## DOMESTICATING MY GORILLA.

 HAD my men build a strong cage of bamboo, and in it I put the little beggar on a bed of dried leaves. This was no easy job, for, his first fright over, the fierce little brute distributed right and left cuffs and bites, until the ingenious Thursday hit on a way of somewhat disarming him. While two men held him down and a third pinioned his head in a crotch, Thursday cut his claws short. His teeth were now his only weapons of attack; but of these he made right good use, as many of the men's legs and arms can testify.

Thursday thinking it necessary to name him, I selected " Joseph," by antithesis; for the great men in history who have borne this name have been models of gentleness, and my young friend could hardly be said to follow their illustrious example. During the first days of his captivity I gave him the purest water, the finest bananas, fragrant leaves, and pineapples. But in vain; he would touch nothing. But one fine morning I found that his supply of food had been materially reduced and that his water-butt was empty. Hunger had evidently got the better of his obstinacy, and I thought it an opportune moment to begin to accustom him to my presence and voice.

When he saw me he drew back into the furthest corner of his cage growling and showing his teeth; and when I went round the outside of his prison, every time that I came near him he would spring across to the other side, and if I put my hand between the bars to stroke him he darted with open mouth at it, and I had just time to withdraw it quickly to avoid his terrible fangs.

In spite of his youth his set of teeth was complete, and he only lacked strength of jaw to be dangerous. One morning, while trying to escape, — an attempt which he made whenever the cage was opened, — he bit a piece out of a man's shoulder, wounding him severely.

He never ate except at night; and finding I was accomplishing nothing, and not wishing to end my days at Stromby, I decided to change my tactics and try starvation. When I saw he was growing thin with hunger I again approached him with bits of wild sugar-cane and young pineapple plants, of which I had noticed he was exceedingly fond. He watched me, growling as before, but I noticed he glanced with a certain longing at the fruit I offered him, and I felt confident of final success. Sure enough, after several hours of repeating this offer Joseph came softly to the end of the cage where I stood, put his arm outside, and grabbed a piece of sugar-cane, retiring immediately to the other side, where he ate it. The next day he satisfied his hunger, taking everything

that I offered him direct from my hand, but not allowing
me to touch him any more than on the previous days.
Wishing to pass my hand along the tawny hair of his

HUNTING A GORILLA.

back, he made a vicious bite at my hand which I only just
escaped. And this was all I could obtain. As long as I
had food for him he would remain near, but when I had

nothing further to offer him he drew back growling and making fearful faces.

One day, while they were changing his bed, he sprang upon the negro as he opened the cage, bit him cruelly, and darted out. I saw it all, but it happened so quickly that I had no time to interfere, while Joseph made tracks for the woods. I set up a shout; and the natives, armed with stones and javelins, arranged themselves in line across his way. When he saw he could not get through, he made a dash for a lofty tree which shot its straight trunk ninety feet into the air, and began to climb it,— with less agility than he would have displayed if Thursday had not cut his claws, but still quickly enough to be out of reach before the natives could get to the foot of the tree. I watched him go up, not without a certain amount of curiosity, as from time to time he stopped to growl at us and then, with a defiant glance, go on. When he reached the top of the tree he hid in the clump of foliage that crowned it, and gave no sign of life. One of the natives offered, for a small reward, to go up after him; and as I had not yet given up all hope of success, I promised it him. The negro began to climb, slowly enough, the slippery trunk, and all went well for the first half of the way. Round his waist he carried one of my fish-nets, which, when he reached the top, he thought he could easily throw over the gorilla, and catch him without serious risk to himself. When he had climbed a little over half way up, we saw the young gorilla come out of his hiding-

A STRUGGLE FOR LIFE.

place, and leaning far out and holding on by a branch, watch the movements of his advancing enemy. The sight was an odd one, and, as I heard Joseph's furiously rumbling growls I began to see that the negro had undertaken no easy task. At a given moment he received about his head and shoulders all the fruit that master Joseph could pluck from the tree, which in a few moments he had completely despoiled, leaving himself without further ammunition. The native had dodged a large part of the missiles by circling the tree, and as most of the fruit was overripe, he suffered but little damage. When the gorilla could find nothing further to throw he again took refuge in the leafy top, uttering cries of rage which promised a warm reception to his pursuer when the latter should come within reach of his sharp teeth. The native moved cautiously upward, for he was within a few feet of the swaying top, and the gorilla had shown no sign. It was at once exciting and amusing. The gorilla might spring upon his enemy, who, under the shock and pain from a bite, might lose his hold and come toppling down a hundred feet or so upon the ground. Luckily there was no such tragic ending. At the very moment when the hunter cast the net over the topmost branch, upon which Joseph had perched, the latter with the quickness of thought slid down the trunk on the other side, and amid a shout of laughter from the crowd beneath, hung a few yards below his pursuer. It took the poor fellow fully half an hour to disentangle his net caught in the multifarious branches. while the gorilla watched him coolly. When the former began to descend the latter did the same.

“We have him.” cried I. making signs to the men to silently surround the base of the tree.

“Not yet. massa.” replied the less sanguine Thursday, whose doubt was justified by wily Joseph. who, seeing the unfriendly circle immediately below him, went rapidly up the tree again, avoiding the would-be captor’s net. and, in fact, climbing directly over his body without wasting time to bite him as he went, and again taking up his old quarters in the very top of the tree. The native renewed his pursuit. and the same comedy was repeated several times. until. from sheer exhaustion, the chase had to be abandoned.

The king. however. suggested a stratagem which proved successful. Guarding the tree till night we stretched our net around the base of the tree, with a man in hiding holding its lines. Joseph. thinking the field clear. came down from his perch. was forthwith captured, thrashed. and put back into his cage. Thursday confided to me that this wretched little monster must be bewitched by an evil spirit and that I could never tame it. Whatever the cause. his conclusion was certainly correct. In spite of all my care and watchfulness I could do nothing with his savage habits. Indeed, captivity seemed to add each day to his intractability and ferocity. He had come to know me. and when he saw me going by and was hungry he called me with a cry pitched to a special key which he used for me alone. But woe to me if I happened to get too near him! He would make a quick snatch at my arm or leg. and I nearly always left a piece of my clothing in his possession. I saw clearly that these coverings were not what he was really after, and that he would gladly have buried his teeth in my flesh,— an end which I took precious good care he should not accomplish.

Every day the king repeated to me his certainty that I could do nothing with the brute, and that, as had been proved time and again by the natives, he was sure to die within a month. On the twenty-first day of his captivity Joseph refused all food. crouching in one corner of his cage. his eyes dull and mournful. seeming to regard everything that went on round him without the least interest. He seemed to be suffering from a violent fever, for every few minutes he would dart to his water-butt and drain it to the last drop. Now I could touch him without his trying to bite me. It even looked as if he regarded me, from his dim, half-closed eyes, with less fierceness, and I felt a kind of remorse at having deprived the poor fellow of his free forest life. I took him out of his cage and laid him on a bed of moss and leaves in the sunlight, and he allowed me to do so. like a child, without making any attempt to escape or bite. It was the fifth day of his sickness when he began to toss about restlessly, and every now and then was seized with a fit of

choking which left him without strength or motion on his
bed of pain. The natives advised me to get rid of him at
once, several even offering themselves to kill him for me;
but I declined. He was too human in his sufferings. In
spite of his weakness, he had kept in the highest degree
his instinct of self-preservation; and at the slightest movement near him his eye would suddenly flash again, as it
used when any one approached him. He seemed, curiously enough, to fear the blacks much more than me.
I surrounded him with every care and attention I could
think of, convinced that if he recovered he would never
resume toward me his natural ferocity. But it was of
no use; he sank hour by hour, and on the ninth day his
death-agony began. I shall never forget the painful last
half-hour. Poor Joseph, his head on my knees, trembling with cold, although the temperature was eighty,
began to show those signs of approaching death which,
once seen, can never be forgotten. The silence and
solitude around me, only one of my race within many
miles, and the night of the black forests of southern
Africa no doubt all contributed to give more importance
than it deserved to this pathetic sight. I had lived in
India and other countries where they believe in metemp-
sychosis, so many years, — countries where the right of animals to live is almost as much respected as that of man,
— that it may have had a great effect on my thoughts and
ideas. But I could not help wondering, as this poor
animal, so human in his death-throes, lay in my arms,

POOR JOSEPH, HIS HEAD ON MY KNEES.

whether man, who cannot create a spear of grass, has the right to destroy life in all its forms around him, more often to satisfy his whim than his necessity; and whether it really is his rôle here below to be continually breaking those infinitely fine links of the chain of destiny which binds together all beings, all spheres, and all worlds.

The next day I had the body buried at the foot of a great tree, and made my preparations for departure, thinking all the while, in spite of myself, of certain theories of modern anthropologists, and wondering if I had interrupted the development of a primate into a human being. After a few hours' march I laughed at the idea, but still I have always retained a singular recollection of Joseph's death, so like that of a young child.

Aside from all question of sentiment, and to return to the more healthy one of science, I may say, after due inquiry and experiment, that I do not believe the gorilla can be domesticated. There is such a wild strain of ferocity in his nature that man's mind can have no influence on it. I tried a similar experiment on an older gorilla which, so far as results went, proved the same as the one I have already described, except that the subject finally escaped. What might be the effect of confining a pair of gorillas and bringing up their offspring in the cage with them, I cannot say. After several generations had been brought up in bondage there might be something accomplished. But I consider it a fact beyond question that the young gorilla cannot be tamed, and as for capturing him alive when older it is as impossible as to lay violent hands on the Bengal tiger or the African lion; to the latter, indeed, he may fairly be compared. It is

I HAD THE BODY BURIED AT THE FOOT OF A TREE.

an undoubted fact that the lion, so common in other parts of Africa, is very rarely found where the gorilla is. They are no match for these terrible enemies, and they run to cover and hide when his roars re-echo through the forests. Even the elephant gets such blows and bites from him that, the natives say, although he is able to cope with him, he prefers not to fight. In the order of primates and even in his own family of anthropoids, the gorilla occupies a place apart and seems to deserve a special family for himself. We have finished with this interesting and mysterious animal, which, looking only at his physical structure, is the being, in nature, nearest like man.

# CHAPTER V.

## HUNTING CHIMPANZEES.

IN this same family of anthropoids the chimpanzee, after the gorilla. is the monkey most resembling man. He climbs with much greater ease than the gorilla, and can stand as straight as he; but when he wishes to move he is obliged to fall on all fours, where the gorilla usually walks in an upright position. Although of a savage enough nature, especially when full grown, the chimpanzee is readily tamed, and in this way more than makes up for his physical inferiority to the gorilla. He is as intelligent, gentle, and social in his instincts as the other is stupidly fierce. And where the latter is more like man in stature and build. the former resembles him even more in the quickness of his intelligence and the gentleness of his ways, after domestication. When wild he is very industrious. building stout shelters for himself in tall trees twenty-five or thirty feet from the ground, and never on it like the gorilla. And, different again from the latter, he is fond of climbing. and his gymnastic exercises would make a professional acrobat jealous. On my voyage up the Niger and on the shores of Guinea I saw crowds of these animals, and

nearly always hanging from the top branches of the highest trees, whence they watched me with wonder mingled with fear. At the slightest movement on my part they fled headlong, making dizzy leaps from branch to branch. ending in running to cover in their huts, from which nothing would tempt them. These shelters are usually in the crotch between two branches, and are made of bamboo. interwoven. and bound together and to the tree very cleverly with withes. The roof is rounded like those of the natives' huts. which, indeed. in all respects. it is not unlike. One curious thing that I have often noticed is that they choose a tree at a little distance from its neighbors. so that no animal can use the branches of other trees as drawbridges to the chimpanzee's fortress. The approach can be made only by the trunk of the very tree in which the hut is built; and there is no funnier sight than to see a family of chimpanzees surprised a little way from home. and making for it on the double-quick. Up goes the mother first. one or two of her youngest clinging to her neck; if there is a young one say two or three years old, he follows next, slowly and uttering cries of distress, until, as his strength nearly gives out and he begins to slip back. his mother throws one of her long arms back and grasps him. places him on her shoulder. where he hangs in desperation, and she continues her ascent with this addition to her precious burden. Meanwhile the male has remained at the base of the tree to defend his family on their retreat, showing his teeth at all comers in a way meant to be terrifying, but which is only comic. As soon as his mate is in safety he takes *his* turn in climbing the tree, at a tremendous pace, and hiding in his hut. Now keep perfectly quiet, and you will soon see a most charming sight. Hearing nothing further, the male soon sticks out his naturally surprised-looking phiz and looks around with an inquisitive glance. Nothing to be seen — evidently the enemy has departed; the soft breeze gently waves the palm leaves, the gray squirrels bound from branch to branch, and the great white herons fan the air with heavy, silent wings; the danger has passed, and the moment for enjoyment has come. At the door of his aerial house stands the chimpanzee uttering little encouraging calls to his family; then, with the grace of a gymnast and an unequalled strength, he seizes the end of the nearest branch and swings himself off, as on a trapeze, hanging by one hand, and with a leap is in the top of the tree, where his mate and such of the young as are strong enough promptly join him. Then the party indulges in the wildest gambols and the forest resounds with their joyful cries.

Our climate is not favorable to the chimpanzee, and it is with great difficulty that they are kept alive in our menageries. They always succumb sooner or later to a trouble of the stomach. Although so easily taught when young, they seem as they grow older to lose this characteristic, and become cross and unsociable, so much so that they often have to be killed. I saw one once be-

AT THE DOOR OF HIS AERIAL HOUSE STANDS THE CHIMPANZEE.

longing to a trader of Formosa that really was remarkably well taught and intelligent. After that fatal voyage up the Niger. when I left two thirds of my party buried on its banks, I spent nearly two months with this trader. a Swiss by birth. who had spent years on the African coast. It was here that I made the acquaintance of Master Jack, a fine specimen of his race, — tall, with silky black hair, dashed with a little white on his belly, and with a bare, shiny face that seemed always well shaven. Although the chimpanzee generally finds an upright position uncomfortable and seldom indulges in it, Jack had acquired the accomplishment of standing and walking ; and his spinal column had finally developed on that axis until he preferred a vertical position to that usually assumed by his race. His ears were large but well formed, his forehead arched and high, and his hands very like a man's, and with nails carefully trimmed by his native keeper, who was at once his original captor and teacher. Like all well brought-up chimpanzees, Master Jack had several domestic accomplishments. He waited at table like a born butler, would pour you wine or water at a word, carry the empty plates away. and all with an amusing, evident enjoyment of his work and an address and silence that most of the heavy-footed native waiters would have done well to imitate.

There was one duty, however. that it would not do to trust to him, — that of bringing in the fruit at dessert. His training had rather added to than diminished his

natural gluttony. and once when he had been called upon
for this service he was still gorging himself with the
rarest grapes as he brought in his master's fruit-dish
filled with pineapples and bananas from which he had
stolen them.  Sometimes. indeed. when he was not being
watched. he would walk off with the whole dish, hiding
it in his bamboo hut that had been built for him in the
court-yard. and coming back into the dining-room, now
and then licking his chops over some of his plunder.
This ceased to be amusing when. instead of taking native
fruits that could be easily replaced. he stole a magnificent
basket of apples and pears that had been sent his master
from France for a dinner party.  The loss was not discovered till the day after the fruit's arrival. when only an
empty basket remained in the hut to prove the thief.
I suffered myself from the rascal's gluttony. in a way
which did his cleverness so much credit that I must
tell it.  I was in the habit of taking every morning at
daybreak a cup of very strong black coffee and a sandwich, which my own favorite man always laid on a table
at the head of my bed. and then turning over for another
nap in the cool of the morning. which. in that climate.
follows the oppressive heat of the night.  I always heard
my faithful Thursday. who was still with me, come in
and leave the cup where I could reach it, and I had
become so used to the operation that. without opening
my eyes. I would after a little while stretch out my
hand mechanically and get the fragrant draught, almost

without disturbing my rest. When I did not eat the sandwich, as was often the case, I would save it for Master Jack.

One fine morning I put out my hand as usual, but no coffee was there, although I had certainly heard Thursday bring it in a few minutes before. I forgot to speak to him about it during the day, and the next morning the same thing occurred. Thursday came at his regular hour, and two minutes later the coffee had disappeared. I suspected a little darky who brought me my morning bath, and resolved to surprise him in the act and teach him a lesson. The following day when Thursday brought in my tray, he woke me as I had instructed him, and I lay with half-closed eyes ready to jump up at the slightest sound. At the end of five minutes, hearing nothing, I ventured a glance at the bamboo stand, when what was my astonishment to see the cup was empty! And I had heard and seen no one! I called Thursday.

"Where is Tom?" said I. That was the little darky's name.

"I saw him just now in the kitchen, massa."

"You did not see him come upstairs?"

"No, massa. Has Tom taken anything belonging to you?"

"Look," said I, pointing to the table. "You see, my coffee is gone!"

Thursday did not grasp the situation. "Has not massa taken his coffee this morning?" he inquired blandly.

"No, nor yesterday, nor the day before."

His great eyes open, his lower jaw dropped, Thursday stood thunderstruck.

"You see," I added, "there is no one in the house beside Tom to do such a thing."

Recovering a little from his surprise, the kindly fellow shook his head slowly and said, —

"No, it can't be Tom, for he went at four o'clock with the cook to get the fish, and is but just returned. He had not taken off his basket when massa called me."

This seemed proof conclusive of his innocence; but who could be the sly thief?

"Would massa like to know who has played him this trick?" Thursday whispered, making the strangest faces and gestures. "It is the mafoucs!"

"Who the deuce are they?"

"They are the evil spirits of the Niger, who are furious at not having been able to kill the white chief who invaded their shores, and have come to revenge themselves here."

I could not help laughing at his superstitious fears.

"My good Thursday," I said, "that I am not buried in their marshes is due to your devotion and my own capital constitution. As for these mafoucs —"

"Speak no evil of them, sir," he urged, with real terror; and I concluded to let the matter rest until I could catch the thief unaided. At dinner I told the story to my host, who smiled in a knowing way, and, to my question as to whether he could solve the mystery, laughingly replied, " I think so.   It must be Jack."

" Your chimpanzee?"

" None other."

" I can't believe it."

" Well, all you have to do is never to lose sight of the cup of coffee to-morrow after it is set on the table."

I resolved to follow his suggestion.

At the usual hour Thursday brought my coffee, and I lay with half-closed eyes watching the cup intently. I had to wait but a few moments before the superstitions of my servant seemed about to be justified.   The cup and saucer began to move from the centre toward the edge of the table without any apparent cause!   I sat up quickly, and the mysterious agent and his methods were revealed to my astonished eyes.   Crouching behind the table, which hid him as the cup did his hand, was Jack, who must have stolen in on all fours, so that I should not see him, with an expression of prospective delight on his greedy face that was comic.   He was so intent on his errand that he did not notice me at first, until I uttered an exclamation of pleasure at catching the rascal red-handed.   Then, seeing Thursday blocking the door at which he had entered, he sprang to a ventilator, always open in this sultry climate, and with the greatest ease and agility swung himself out on to the eaves, and so into a neighboring tree.   Safe in his improvised fortress, he hurled down upon us all the branches he could reach and break off, chattering and making faces at us as only a chimpanzee can. The voice of his owner brought him down at last, and we soon became fast friends.

The most surprising part of the whole thing was Jack's remarkable quickness of apprehension, and his choice of alternatives — always hitting the better — in reaching a desired end. In fact, one cannot conceive of a trick or clever ruse that he could not fathom and make use of, as was further shown in his strange partnership with a great mastiff of rare strain preserved only in London, from which city one of my host's correspondents had sent him. This animal was a great curiosity in these latitudes, where European dogs seldom live long on account of the heat and especially the diseased food which they find everywhere, and which he had so far avoided by being carefully confined in a large enclosure built for the purpose.

Jack, the rascal, took a fancy to the brute, and finding his taste for the forbidden food, undertook to supply him with bones stolen from the kitchen. In return for this, the mastiff devoted whole days to serving the chimpanzee in the capacity of a pillow; and the latter enjoyed nothing so much as lying at full length on a mat, with his head on his friend's big back.

As I said before, Jack, when found out in his theft, fearing the thrashing he deserved, took refuge in a tree, and was brought to terms only by the sight of his master, who exercised a real fascination over him, and before whom he always acted upon his best behavior. This was because my host had never played with him. nor, although speaking gently to him, petted him. At the same time he never refused him anything to eat which he seemed to want, and this attitude had produced in Jack a certain feeling of respect and fear, mingled with a strong, affectionate attachment.

Beside his fondness for every kitchen dainty, he was also a lover of the cellar and its contents, and an open bottle could not be left anywhere unguarded, without his quick eye observing, and his thirsty lips draining, it. Under the influence of the liquor he would commit the most absurd follies, throwing off all control whatever, and breaking his dishes and belongings, all the time making the most frightful faces and chatterings. Like all tipsy people, he had fixed ideas that nothing would influence, — a favorite one being to climb up the roof of his hut to a pole at the ridge. When this idea seized him. he would creep slowly up the bamboo walls of his hut. clinging by the swellings here and there, until, half-way up. he would lose his grip and go tumbling down upon the ground, to the great amusement of any lookers-on. This he would keep up until. at length, he could reach the top, where. with his arms round the pole, he slept until his brain became clearer of the fumes of wine. Sometimes these bouts had less happy endings. Bottled wines fall an easy prey to the thievish negro servants. and Jack, to satisfy his cravings for liquor, had no scruples in stealing from the thieves any broken cases he could lay his hands on. It was mere play for him to uncork a bottle as well as the butler himself could do it.

IT WAS MERE PLAY FOR HIM TO UNCORK A BOTTLE.

and one morning while I was there he found a hidden treasure, and by eight o'clock was as drunk as a lord. My host was at his office, the ladies not yet risen, and the monkey was at liberty to perform his wildest antics. I was writing at my window, which commanded the court, and looking up, was surprised to see no Jack, but the natives all craning their necks up in my direction. Leaning out of the window, I saw the chimpanzee climbing leisurely up an immense tree and carrying Tom, the little darky, jauntily under his arm. The poor boy, in spite of his friends' advice, shouted up from below, was struggling and weeping, to Jack's evident amusement and delight as he continued his upward course, making the queerest grimaces. Wild with terror, the boy caught at a stout branch, and held on so firmly that the chimpanzee was compelled to stop. This he did, shaking Tom by the heels with his head down, until he was glad to let go and be carried in that position to the topmost branches of the tree. The shouts of the negroes and myself were of no avail; and it was not until I had sent for my friend and he had arrived at the base of the tree, that Jack would bring his prize back to earth and his anxious friends.

A few days later my host said to me at dinner, —

"I am going to make a trip up the Rouyme; don't you want to join me?"

"Why, you know I am only just back from the Niger, and am still chattering with the ague. Could I stand this fatigue so soon?"

"Yes, you have nothing to fear at this season from a new attack, and the fatigue will be slight, as we shall go in a small launch."

"Then I accept with pleasure."

"Although I wanted you to go with me very much, still I should not have urged the trip upon you, except that I knew you were always glad to add to your knowledge of monkeys, and that the country through which this river flows is filled with them in great variety. Two days' sail from here is a forest densely grown with palm and tulip trees festooned with flowering vines, where they love to resort; so much so, indeed, that it is called the Forest of the Monkeys."

"My dear host," I said, "my only anxiety is, *when* do we start?"

"To-morrow, at daybreak."

I summoned my faithful Thursday and told him to get everything ready; for although a short visit to one of his rubber depots was all that my friend had planned, still any journey in Africa means considerable preparation. One must have arms and ammunition, a pocket pharmacopœia,— to preserve at once the health and the skins of game,— and a lot of smaller things that only an old traveller remembers to get beforehand. Long before daylight I was astir, looking over my servant's preparations, and seeing my goods and chattels stowed on board the "Jenny,"— an able little launch, named after my host's charming daughter. The first two days taught us her comforts, as we steamed between the rather monotonous banks, lined with their luxuriant vegetation, and alive with water-rats, vipers, and adders. The trees

HE HELPS HIMSELF TO THE CONTENTS OF THE NATIVES' CALABASHES.

were nearly all the so-called wine-palm, from which the natives get their favorite drink, by tapping, much as we tap sugar-maples. This liquor when drawn off at once is sweet and mild, and not at all disagreeable to a European palate; but after an hour or two of fermentation it becomes absolutely repulsive to all but a negro's taste. From the fruit of this tree a similar, though less valued, drink is obtained, that is very prompt in its effect on the wits of the drinker. This is called the chimpanzee's tree, and it is well named, for the chimpanzee often disputes with man for its possession, and it is in its branches that he builds his clever home. The natives even go so far as to accuse him of helping himself to the contents of their calabashes, hung to catch the " fire-water."

In fact, their stories in relation to this animal, although less savage in their nature than those concerning the gorilla, are no less curious and full of superstition. The native mothers bring up their children on stories like this : —

" One day a chimpanzee met the king's officer. ' Good morning, dealer in slaves,' said he ; ' where are you going, and by what right do you pass through my forest ? ' ' I am going to your majesty's brother, the Sultan Haoussa. who is to sell me two hundred slaves; if your majesty will permit me to pass, I will give you, on my return, six pairs of slaves.' ' All men are liars and cheats,' said the chimpanzee ; ' therefore leave with me your son as hostage.'

Then the officer, standing in great fear of him, left his son and journeyed on. But when he reached the sultan, he said, 'Give me, I pray you, a guard to protect me from the chimpanzee, for I fear lest he may not let me pass again through the forest in safety.' Now, when the animal saw him returning with a large guard, he was very angry, but he hid his wrath and invited them all to eat and drink, and plied them with wine till they were all drunk. Then, taking their lances, he pierced the heart of each soldier, and pinned them all to the ground, and released the slaves. When the officer awoke, the chimpanzee said to him, 'Where are now your guard?' and in revenge for their distrust, he held the officer and his son in slavery ever after."

Of course this is a very simple and naïve fairy-story, but it is interesting as showing the native appreciation of the chimpanzee's intelligence and quite human sense of justice. Indeed, they consider him a man, condemned for his evil deeds to wander for a time under this form, until he shall have expiated his faults.

The second night was upon us in all its impenetrable blackness before we came to anchor. My friend insisted upon my turning in under cover of the cabin, to avoid the damp mists of the river, while he prepared a little theatrical surprise — as he expressed it — for my morning awakening.

" And the scenery?" said I, laughing.

" You will see later.   Do not be worried at our absence, and we will come back for you at the proper moment. Thursday shall stay with you, in case you should want anything."

A plank was thrown ashore, and I heard my friend give his orders in the native tongue, and then leave the boat, followed by his servants.  There was nothing left for me but to roll myself in a blanket and turn in on the cabin lounge.  It was still as dark as Egypt when I was aroused by my host's gentle touch, who said smilingly, " I am sorry to disturb you, but the time has come.  It will be day in an hour."

Thursday had already prepared our tea and buttered toast, and we made a hurried meal before starting for the Forest of Monkeys.  We tramped along in the darkness, feeling our way with great caution, for fully half an hour.  Suddenly the file came to a full stop.

" Here we are," said our guide.  " Take my hand."

He led me to the base of a ladder, which he proceeded to climb, and I after him.  Soon I came to the end of the rounds, and could feel nothing above.

" Where the devil are you taking me ? " said I.

" Don't be afraid, but move this way," he replied.

Following his example, I advanced cautiously until I found myself very comfortably ensconced against a great limb of a banyan, with firm footing beneath me.

" How high from the ground are we ?"

" Oh, not more than ten feet," replied my friend, who

had followed me up the ladder, and now sat down beside me.

"When will you ring up the curtain?" laughed I.

"In a few minutes. Is every one in position?"

"Yes, massa; yes, massa," came from a dozen different branches higher up in the tree.

"All right. Now silence all!"

Day ends and begins in the tropics almost without any twilight, and with the rapidity of a change of scenery at the theatre. Hardly five minutes had elapsed before a pale light struggled through the forest, and in an instant the sun filled the trees with its golden rays, and the day had come.

At a glance I took in the whole remarkable scene. We were perched in the heart of a banyan, sheltered from observation by a screen of palm-leaves, woven together with tough vines and tendrils, yet with an unobstructed view of what was going on around us. At the first light of day, a cry of joy, in a hundred different keys and notes, went up from the innumerable little huts hanging, like grapes in cluster, from every tree in the forest. Each of these huts sheltered its family of chimpanzees, and old and young came bounding out, uttering piercing cries, to join in a grand romp. Thousands of the agile animals sprang from branch to branch of the highest trees, balancing, swinging, leaping, sliding, and making a weird scene to my eyes, unaccustomed to see so large a number of monkeys at once. We stayed nearly two hours, watching their play, and we were so completely hidden that none of them suspected our presence. After seeing them in this way, I became convinced that the natives' opinion of their intelligence, and their obedience to the recognized chiefs of their strange communities, is justified by the facts. This city of theirs proves their social instinct, and its very existence makes certain tacit rules of conduct probable. It is this social life that especially distinguishes the chimpanzee from the gorilla, who lives only with his family and never in communities.

# CHAPTER VI.



I MAKE THE ACQUAINTANCE OF THE ORANG-OUTANG.

T was not till some months after the incidents mentioned in the last chapter that I found an opportunity to study another species of the animal most nearly resembling man, — the orang-outang.

This monkey is found in Borneo, and thither Thursday — now grown more civilized and more indispensable — and I turned our faces. We took passage on a craft going out with Chinese laborers, and a hard voyage we had of it, with head winds and a heavy sea. But at last, ten days late. we arrived at Saraouak. and immediately inquired of the native hunters where we could best find the game for which we were in search. They advised the Sadong River. running to the east from Saraouak, and bordered its entire length with dense forests. I hired a Dyak porter to carry our provisions. and we set out. Two days later we were floating on the river. and my ardent desire was about to be gratified.

Orang-outang is a word meaning in Borneo " Man-of-the-Forest." and is applied to what is now a species of small stature. rarely five feet high. but of stalwart build,

the body being often in circumference two thirds of the
height.  His arms are a quarter longer than his legs, so
that when travelling on all fours his attitude is half up-

AN ORANG-OUTANG.

right; but he never really stands on his legs like a man,
popular belief to the contrary notwithstanding.  When
young his color is tawny, but he grows black with years.

The orangs live in couples in the most secluded parts of the forest, and are never active, like the chimpanzees, but sit all day with their legs round a branch, their heads forward in the most uncomfortable attitude, occasionally uttering mournful sounds. When pursued they climb slowly up a tree, and at night sleep in the huts built to cover their young, of which they are very careful, and whose wants they supply with almost human tenderness and devotion. When taken young they are susceptible of taming and domesticating, like the chimpanzee, but as they grow older they become cross and violent, and, curiously enough, the forehead — prominent in the adult — becomes retreating in later years.

After waiting some days without seeing any orangs, my native guide advised our going away from the river, deeper into the unbroken forest; and this we did, a two days' march. One morning, just as I had killed and was examining a queer wild pig, I heard a rustling in the leaves over my head, and looking up, was paralyzed with surprise to see, some twenty-five or thirty feet above me, an enormous orang-outang quietly seated on a tamarind branch, watching me and grinding his teeth. My porter was making me elaborate signals of distress, which Thursday translated into advice to shoot the beast, who was old and fully grown, with my explosive-ball rifle.

" He says he is an evil one," added Thursday, " and that the old orangs are very dangerous and will attack a man at sight."

A DYAK OF BORNEO.

"All right," I replied. "If he offers to attack us, I will stop him promptly with a bullet."

It is true that one of my most ardent desires was to obtain a skeleton of a fully developed orang-outang, but I decided to postpone the gratification of it until I should have watched the animal's movements in a state of absolute freedom. I told my men to clap their hands and shout, to scare him, but all he did was to sit and grind his teeth; and I was almost persuaded to try my Dyak's advice, when the orang-outang coolly grasped a branch hanging near, and swung himself slowly from tree to tree without any apparent effort, about as fast as we could walk beneath. We followed him until the dense undergrowth made the path impracticable. An athlete would have performed this trapeze act with, perhaps, more grace, but nothing could surpass the indolent ease with which he left us behind.

This was my first interview with this peculiar animal; and the superstitious Dyak assured Thursday, relating numerous parallel cases, that as I had not killed the orang, the orang would certainly kill me. He said he had known a great many travellers who had been attacked by them and killed, and that I would soon join their number, although he confessed that he had never himself been present at such a misfortune.

One morning, as I was returning from a long walk through the woods in search of insects, one of my boys came running toward me, shouting with excitement. "Quick. take your gun! a large orang. a large orang!"

He had only breath enough left to tell me the animal was up the path toward the Chinaman's camp. and I hurried in that direction. followed by two Dyaks. One barrel of my gun was loaded with ball, and I sent Charley — the boy — back to camp for more ammunition, in case I should find the game had kindly waited for me. We walked carefully. making almost no noise. stopping every now and then to look round ourselves. until Charley rejoined us at the spot where he had seen the orang, and I put ball in the other barrel and waited, sure that we were near the game. In a moment or two I heard a heavy body moving from tree to tree. but the foliage was so thick we could see nothing. Finally, fearing I might lose him entirely. I fired at guess into a tree in which we thought he must be. For so large an animal he moved with remarkable swiftness and silence, but I felt sure. if we could follow his general course. we should eventually catch sight of him in some more open bit of forest. And so it proved. Just at the spot where he had first been seen by Charley, and to which we had now got back. his tawny side and black head appeared for an instant. long enough for me to give him both barrels; and while I was reloading I saw him cross the path. dragging one leg as if it had been broken by my shot. At any rate. he could not use it. and he took refuge between two branches of a lofty tulip-tree. sheltered from sight by the thick

THEY ARE VERY CAREFUL OF THEIR YOUNG.

growth of glossy leaves. I was afraid he would die up there, and I should never get him or his skeleton. It was no use trying to get the Dyaks to climb the tree and

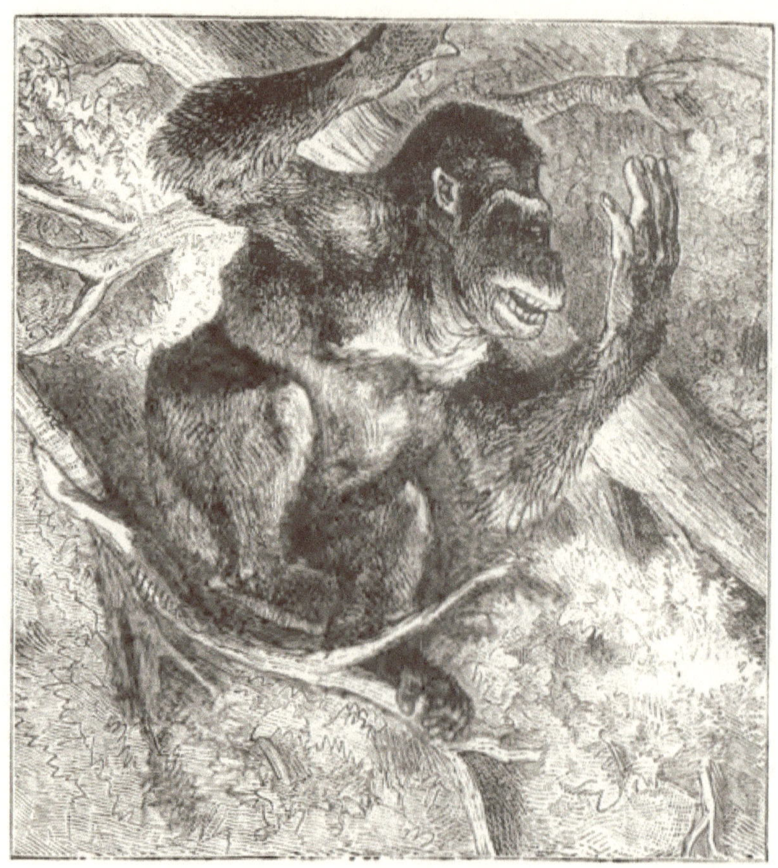

HE TOOK REFUGE BETWEEN TWO BRANCHES OF A LOFTY TREE.

cut the branch from under him ; they were afraid, and said so. We tried to dislodge him with all sorts of missiles, but in vain. Finally we started to cut down the tree ; but when the trunk was severed the tree only leaned over, and was held in that position by innumerable tough vines running to a dozen neighboring trees. It would take us all night to cut them all down ; still, we began the work, which almost immediately gave the tree such a shaking that down came the gigantic orang with a tremendous thud. When we came to measure him, we found him a giant indeed, stretching from hand to hand over six feet. He was horribly wounded, — both his legs broken, a bullet in his neck, another in his jaw, and a whole joint shot away from the base of his spinal column. And yet he was alive ! When he fell the Chinamen lashed him to a litter and carried him into camp, where it took Charley and myself all day to clean his skin and boil the flesh from his skeleton. From this and many similar experiences I have become convinced that, in spite of stories to the contrary, the orang-outang never attacks man. His policy is always flight, and to my own testimony is added that of all the Chinese wood-cutters whom I met in Borneo ; and the island is full of them.

The next day, while looking for material to make myself a table for natural history specimens, Thursday and I ran across an old camp of some of these Chinese lumbermen, where fragments of plank and scantling were plenty. While we were gathering these I chanced to look up in the tree above us, and into the eyes of a very large orang-outang whose head only was visible. Remembering the skeleton I wanted, I raised my rifle

THE CHINAMEN'S CAMP.

immediately and fired where I knew the body must be. The animal, wounded but not killed, fell heavily to the ground, but almost at once started toward a neighboring tree, from which Thursday and a Dyak headed him off. Although badly wounded, the brute would have been more than a match for them both, had not a second shot from me ended the struggle.

It proved to be a fully grown female, and a tiny young one was clinging to her in terror. Had I known this circumstance I should not have harmed her, but it was too late then to make any difference. The little fellow trembled in every limb when Thursday brought him to me, and, in spite of my caresses, would not be reassured. But the more difficult it seemed to do anything with him, the more I resolved to succeed, and remembering my experience with the young gorilla, I set about devising some way of feeding him. I started the Dyak off in search of a goat, and told him not to return until he found one. Meanwhile I mixed sugar, bread, and water together, and, although at first he declined it energetically, he soon sucked it from my finger with a decided gusto. It proved, however, too strong food for so young a stomach, and I was just beginning to think he would die on my hands, when the Dyak, followed by a Chinaman and a goat. came into camp. The Chinaman should have been a Jew, so sharp was he at trading; but finally, after pretending that I cared nothing whatever about his goat, and after long haggling on his part, starting at one hundred rupees (twelve dollars and fifty cents) and coming down to five, the goat became mine, and the little orang-outang obtained a step-mother that soon rivalled its own mother in tenderness. She nursed it and caressed it exactly as if it had been her own. and a very pretty sight it was. He soon grew large enough to travel on his own sturdy legs, at any sudden alarm running quickly back to his nurse and clinging to her with his sinewy fingers.

When he strayed away out of her sight in the woods. it was really pathetic to hear her bleatings and his answering cries. He had gradually come to know me, and he treated us all with the greatest gentleness. When he was three months old I began to give him bananas, of which he was very fond, and he afterward became accustomed to other fruits ; but nothing ever pleased him like the goat's milk. He learned very quickly, and at five months knew all objects in my tent by name, bringing to me anything I called for, which was certainly more than many children of two or even three years could have done. But with the latter, development progresses with giant strides after that age, while with an orang it ceases. What an animal is at one year of age he always remains.

One morning a Chinaman came to offer for sale a tiny monkey which he had partially tamed. This little animal looked like a pygmy beside my young orang, but he could do a variety of things, like feeding himself, etc., that the larger was not yet up to. So I bought him,

THE BRUTE, ALTHOUGH BADLY WOUNDED, WOULD HAVE BEEN MORE THAN A MATCH FOR THEM.

and put them in the same hut, where they soon became fast friends; the monkey, on account of his more perfectly developed faculties, being easily master.

When he wanted to sleep nothing would do but that the orang must lie down too, and let him pillow his head on him. But there was another side to this; for the orang-outang looked upon him as a kind of doll, invented for his particular enjoyment. and when he felt in playful mood, he would seize the monkey by the ear or the neck or the tail, and swing him round and hold him in any uncomfortable position at his own sweet will. The monkey would rage and even weep, but only interference on our part would stop this rough treatment. He learned early, as all animals do, to distinguish the members of our party and their relations, and, as master, he always treated me with respectful obedience. I taught him to eat rice boiled in milk, and to use a spoon and bowl like his little friend, who, by the way, was fond of stealing from him all he safely could. They were both gluttons, and nothing amused Thursday more than to set them quarrelling over some bit of choice fruit. As the orang's teeth grew. his temper and character became more pronounced, and, like an ill brought-up child, he wished all round him to give way to his whims. He had no consideration whatever for the Dyak, who washed and tended him with the greatest patience, but tried to pull his hair and bite him whenever the mood seized him. I named him Joseph and the monkey Jack. — after my chimpanzee

friend, — and they answered promptly to their names
when called. without mistake.   I was proud of them and
their accomplishments. and tempted to send them home

to some naturalist. but chance prevented.   You should
have seen them, — Jack. a napkin round his neck. seated
at a corner of the table eating slowly with fork and spoon,

like any well-taught child; Joseph, with a napkin over
his arm, waiting upon him as solemnly as an English
butler.  To be sure, they stole the best fruit — but then,
no one is perfect!  It was with a real pang that I left
these little fellows behind with a friend, to whom I gave
them on my departure from Borneo.

Perhaps this is the only case on record of the growth
in captivity of a young orang-outang, and it is interesting
to note in what ways he resembled a child.  When very
young he lay nearly always on his back, with his legs in
the air, and when he wanted anything he simply put his
head back and howled till he got it.  When he first began
to walk it was with the same timid hesitation that a child
does, and when he succeeded in taking a few steps without falling, he glanced at us with a very human look of
triumph.  The appearance of the goat always caused him
a high degree of satisfaction, expressed, again like a child
on the entrance of its mother, by little sighs of contentment.  I may say, indeed, that up to the age of four or
five months I saw nothing different in him from what
I have remarked in a child except that difference of
development mentioned before.

My stay in Borneo was coming to an end when one
morning I set out on a hunting trip which proved well-
nigh my last.  I carried my smooth twenty-four bore
and, in deference to the Dyaks' urgent appeals, my rifle
with its explosive ammunition.

"It is a dangerous neighborhood," one of them said,

"and we are liable to meet a tiger." This caution proved my safety, and without it I should not now be reeling off these veracious experiences, although we met no tigers.

WE WERE TRAVELLING THROUGH THE EDGE OF A GREAT SWAMP.

Up the Sadong we paddled for nearly an hour, until the trees along its banks began to grow thinner and a decided change in the character of the shores became apparent.

We were travelling through the edge of a great swamp where peat pits and stagnant pools alternated strangely with little oases of clustered trees, contrasting sharply with the surrounding level and looking for all the world like floating islands.

We landed and began a careful march across the quaking ground toward one of the larger islands. The soft mud showed recent tracks of orang-outangs, some of them evidently of the largest size. It was a long and difficult tramp, and my heart began to misgive me that the Dyaks had misled me in promising good sport before night-fall, when the leader of our file stopped suddenly in the greatest apparent excitement and terror.

"What is it?" said I to Thursday, sternly. "Let us have no nonsense."

"He says he has made a mistake, and that the tide is rising."

"Well, what of it? There is n't tide enough here to drown a dog. Tell him to go on."

And on we went, to the Dyak's intense disgust and soon to our own apprehension; for, although the tide rises but little, it soon covered our path, raised but little from the surrounding marsh, and made advance or retreat at first dangerous and then impossible! I was very angry with the rascal, but decided to take it out of him later, when we should be out of our unpleasant predicament, and to bear the discomfort of standing in water up to the knees for a few hours with what philosophy I could muster. Suddenly the scene. which had its comic side, assumed a tragic one. I was trying to distinguish, along the horizon. the point where the ocean began, when I heard an exclamation of horror from the natives, who, with eyes starting from their sockets. pointed eastward toward the nearer tree clumps.

"What is it?" said I. straining my eyes in the same direction, but in vain.

"Crocodiles! Crocodiles!"

I repeated the word mechanically. my heart sinking within me as I, too, began to distinguish the black points which indicated to the Dyaks' quick eyes the approaching enemy.

"Are you sure?" I whispered hoarsely. the cold sweat pouring off my forehead.

"Yes. Sahib, certain; and there are four of them."

I had only six explosive-ball cartridges. and. in spite of their terrible effectiveness. I could but remember that the crocodile in the water is well-nigh invulnerable. with only his armor-plated back exposed. However. the terrible foe was still some way off. and I should not myself have detected them but for the Dyaks' quick instinct. There was nothing left us but to try, at any cost, to reach the nearest of the tree islands, avoiding by guess the bottomless mud-holes that beset the path.

The unfortunate Dyak who was responsible for our position headed the line again, sounding to right and left, as he advanced, with his spear. It is impossible to

"CROCODILES! CROCODILES!"

describe this adventure, — marching through the water, pursued by crocodiles, not daring to put down one's foot until assured by sounding that it would reach something solid. Although the island grew perceptibly nearer, our hungry neighbors did too, and at an increasing pace. Still we were distancing them, — for over many of the shoals they could not swim, and wading, for a crocodile, is a slow process, — when, without warning, and as quick as lightning, we felt the ground sink beneath our feet, and we were all four precipitated simultaneously into the swamp. Instinctively, Thursday and I raised our weapons and ammunition high over our heads, for when we touched bottom — that is, a fairly solid layer of vegetable matter — the water reached our arm-pits.

"We might as well give up," said I, in despair; "this time we are lost!"

"Oh, don't give up yet, Sahib. We are so low that, with this head wind, the crocodiles cannot see us and will perhaps be unable to find us at all. Let us cover our heads with these marsh grasses and leaves and 'lie low.'"

His advice was so evidently good that instead of a vain attempt to reach the firm land with its inevitable exposure to the hungry eyes of our terrible pursuers, we acquiesced at once. After several minutes of suspense, the Dyak raised himself slightly on a hummock, and glanced cautiously toward the spot where we had last seen them. His face cleared at once, and he cheered us with. —

"They have lost us, and have separated to search for us. Three are going almost directly away from this place, and one only knows enough to keep on in the first course."

WE COVERED OUR HEADS WITH MARSH-PLANTS.

"And he is headed for us?"

"In a straight line!"

"Then do not lose sight of him for an instant.   With

one enemy we may be able to cope, and then there is a chance that he may lose the scent."

When I asked him again where the animal was, — for I dared not raise my own head to look, — he replied that he was still coming straight toward us, and I saw that a meeting was inevitable and made my preparations accordingly.

I took my rifle from Thursday and loaded it with an explosive ball, and gave him my hunting-piece instead.

"Now then, Thursday," said I, "listen to my instructions. The Dyak says the crocodile is sure to find us. I shall let him get within ten yards of us, and then I shall fire at whatever vulnerable part I can, — his eye or his belly. Of course I may miss him, or the bullet may glance off his back without wounding him."

The black's eyes rolled with horror.

"Then, without an instant's hesitation and yet without haste, you, who must stand just behind me, must take my rifle and hand me my other gun for a second shot. Do you understand?"

"Perfectly."

"And I can depend on you?"

"Till death."

"We will try to make it less bad than *that*, and your courage shall meet its reward."

I knew what he said was true, for the fellow had been devoted to me ever since I saved his life in the jungle when the gorilla grappled him, and I felt I could rely upon him.

Raising myself as high as I could, I took a good look at the slowly approaching monster, and, I confess, a shudder of horror ran through me at his immense size. He was farther off than I had expected, and evidently quite unconscious of our neighborhood, into which he had come by chance, following the raised path on which we ourselves had been travelling when the tide overtook us. I immediately changed my plan of attack. I ordered Thursday to wade off to the left so that the smoke from his gun should not blow across me, and told him to fire at the crocodile and try to wound him, if only slightly. As this would make the latter raise his head and look round, I hoped to get a shot at some very vulnerable spot, and land an explosive ball where it would do most good. I had hardly taken up my position, with rifle lifted, when Thursday's gun cracked sharp and clear, and I saw blood fly from the eye of the crocodile, whose advance ceased immediately. I could hardly restrain a cry of joy, but catching sight of a yellow bit of neck, I fired at it and shut my eyes. A great splash and the shouts of triumph of the Dyaks encouraged me to open them, and I found the success of the shot greater than I could have hoped.

The crocodile lay on his side on a little island with his neck blown open the entire length of the jaw, while the Dyaks, who had made a break for land without regard to Thursday or myself, capered round him. I called them, and they helped me on shore to where the animal lay in his last agony, — for these brutes die as hard as a

THE CROCODILE LAY ON HIS SIDE ON A LITTLE ISLAND.

snake. He was a very large specimen, with a head twice
as long as it was broad, his eyes set close together above
his long snout, of which only the under jaw was movable.
His front feet had five toes armed with claws, and his
hind feet but four, and webbed to allow him to swim
easily. His whole body was shingled with plates of a
shell-like membrane that made him a fine coat of mail
nearly bullet-proof. Green on the back, his color gradually shaded off into yellow, and he was a terrible foe to
meet in the water, where we should not have come off so
well had not our good luck stood by us just as it did.

I was duly thankful to regain the bank, which I had
never expected to touch again, and had not the heart to
blame the Dyak who was responsible for our narrow
escape; but I resolved to place less reliance on the natives
in future.

On the way back, Thursday had the satisfaction of
shooting a fine full-grown orang-outang, without injuring
a bone, and I prepared the skeleton for mounting in an
ingeniously easy way suggested by him. Cutting off the
meat roughly from the frame, we placed the carcass near
a large ant-hill, and surrounded both with a plank fence.
In a week the ants had left it for me clean and white as
ivory. This satisfied me, as far as orang-outangs went,
and I turned next to a lower species of monkey, — the
long-armed ape, or gibbon.

# CHAPTER VII.

## STILL IN BORNEO.

 TRUST the reader will not object to prolonging his stay in Borneo with me, to make the acquaintance of this curious family of apes, owing their name to the unusual proportion of their arms to their legs, as is shown in our picture. They are of a gentle nature and easily tamed, and although less intelligent than their cousins, the chimpanzees and orangoutangs, they are much more agreeable to have anything to do with. As they grow older they seem even more sociable and good-tempered, — quite the opposite, as you see, from the others. They are very common in the forests of India, Java, Sumatra, and Borneo, where they live in large communities under recognized leaders, at whose call they meet at sunrise and sunset, with a fearful din and chattering that must be heard to be appreciated. Even when confined alone, these monkeys retain this habit of greeting the orb of day with a harsh, monotonous cry, repeated when the night comes on, and gaining in intensity and *sending* power — as singers say — through a pocket connected with the larynx in which they can store up air.

A point in which the long-armed ape differs from all
other monkeys, and which therefore must not be forgotten
of them, is their extraordinary care in removing their

THE GIBBON, OR LONG-ARMED APE.

dead far from their homes.  They do this invariably, and
one cannot be long in the vicinity of one of their communities without seeing them engaged in this almost human

errand; four bearers. one for each limb, carrying a dead body toward some quiet spot in the forest.

One night when I was in India I saw a crowd of these gentle creatures climbing over the ruins of an ancient temple, and a weird sight it was. We were passing the night in one of those old brick towers built by the rajahs, at regular distances. to shelter travellers. Imagine a kind of turret twenty or twenty-five feet high. divided into three stories, each of one room surrounded by a low ledge on which travellers might sleep, and crowned with a platform from which they could safely enjoy the comparative coolness of the nights and listen to the strange concert of sounds that arose from the forest round its base. That night the tigers. attracted by our horses that we had stabled in the lower story, prowled round our shelter uttering their penetrating cries. sometimes in a deeper tone that rolled and reverberated like thunder through the tree-tops. To these notes was added the occasional cry of a panther. stealing up to our ill-fastened door to find himself disappointed of his prey. My hunting companion fired his revolver toward several pairs of lurid eyes which. at the report. disappeared into the blackness of the surrounding undergrowth, only to reappear after a few minutes as hungry as ever. A tiger. by the way. is nearly always hungry; for living as he does on the flesh of deer and other swift-footed game. he is often unable to catch them for days together.

One of my friend's shots was followed by an unusually sharp and loud cry.

GENTLE CREATURES CLIMBING OVER THE RUINS.

" Touched," said he.

" Do you think so?"

" Yes, listen."

We could hear the irregular and painful breathing of the beast growing fainter, and in the morning found a few yards from the tower a magnificent specimen of the jaguar with my friend's bullet just back of his shoulder, where death must have followed promptly. On the way back from this very trip we managed to capture a fine, well-grown entellus, that closely resembled the sacred monkey so common in India, especially in Bengal. For this animal the Indians have so deep a veneration that they allow him to enter their gardens and help himself to all the fruit he wants without the least remonstrance. As the animals always travel in companies, this privilege results in absolute starvation to the farmer who is visited. You may go to bed with a superb garden filled with bananas, guavas, and all the delicate tropical fruits, ripe and luscious; the next morning you wake up to find — nothing. At dawn a band of sacred apes has fallen like a blight on your garden; and there the thieves are, eating the plunder under your very nose. The servants refuse to touch the intruders, and if you try to shoot them yourself leave your service, and your house is soon tabooed, for they have the countenance and support of all the superstitious natives from Cape Comorin to the Himalayas and from the Persian Gulf to Calcutta.

The legend from which all this reverence obtains its authority is as follows : —

## THE LEGEND OF RAMA AND THE APE ANNOUMA.

Once upon a time Rama, or Vishnu incarnated under that name, lived in Aodya, passing his youth in the silence of the forests, engaged in meditation and prayer. Djamadogny, King of Militta, having seen some of his wonderful deeds, proposed that he should try to bend an enormous bow, once the property of Siva, the god of war, offering him as reward, if he succeeded, the bow and his beautiful daughter Sita. The latter was so marvellously lovely that all the princes of India had tried to bend the bow, hoping to win her hand, but not one of them could even start it. Rama, without any apparent effort, bent the bow, strung it, and drew the cord an arrow's length, and drove the shaft through the palace walls with such force that it wounded a Brahman's wife within, and so seriously that her life was in danger. Her husband, furious at the accident, by virtue of spells and sorceries uttered a curse that condemned Rama, although a god, to a life in which he should never be wholly successful in anything he undertook, nor perfectly happy. This power is common to all Brahmans, and is irresistible for mortals and gods alike; and poor Rama saw all his undertakings blighted in the bud by this unhappy curse. He had hardly returned with his lovely bride to his own home, where he was now king, when his late father's second wife came to him to beg him to abdicate in favor of her son, alleging that the gods, through the oracle, had declared that to be their wish.

A FEW YARDS FROM THE TOWER A MAGNIFICENT JAGUAR.

Seeing in this another attack from his unhappy fate, Rama laid aside his crown and retired to the forest with his wife Sita and her brother Latchoumana.

One day while the latter was out hunting, he cut off the ears from the six heads of Sauparna, sister of the ten-headed giant Ravana, King of Ceylon. This monarch took his revenge by carrying off Sita one fine afternoon, when her husband and brother were not near to protect her, and immuring her in a dismal dungeon.

Rama was inconsolable at this climax to his misfortunes, and could think of nothing but how he should rescue his beloved wife. To do this an army was necessary, and he applied for aid to the young man in whose favor he had given up his throne, but in vain.

It was now that the apes came to the rescue. Their chief, Annouma, called them together, and put it to vote whether Rama, the incarnation of Vishnu, deserted by gods and men, was not a fit object for sympathy and assistance from them. There was but one sentiment in the meeting, and a messenger was despatched to Ceylon to see what had become of Sita. The extraordinary agility and strength of the ape made him a peculiarly suitable spy, and he succeeded in finding the imprisoned lady, when most men would undoubtedly have failed. When he had reached the castle in which she was confined, he climbed to the top of a tree near her dungeon, and when he saw the fair Sita come on to the terrace to enjoy the fresh evening air, he began to sing her this song : —

> "Of what is the lovely Sita thinking,
> When she looks afar, across the forest,
> She, the daughter of the Earth and Plutus,
> Towards the country of the Sunlight?"

And Sita replied:—

> " I am listening to the breezes
>> From the country of the Sunlight,
>> Bringing words of bitter anguish
>> From my Rama, well-beloved," etc.,

like all the nursery ballads of every people, running on to a great many verses.

The messenger returned to Rama with the assurance that Sita was waiting patiently for his coming with the friendly apes, to free her from the tyrant Ravana. Then Annouma and his allies raised a mighty army of apes, and began to build a bridge of stone over to Ceylon; and while his soldiers brought stone, Annouma uprooted trees and carried rocks, " more than the hairs upon his body." While the bridge was building the bears sent a regiment of their best warriors to reinforce their friends the apes, and together they marched across the bridge toward the centre of Ravana's kingdom.

But he, knowing of their coming, had prepared endless obstructions and legions of opponents. First they were obliged to conquer thousands of crocodiles from the island marshes; then flooded river-beds and mountain torrents opposed them; then came fire, — whole forests sacrificed to the flame. But the brave apes and bears were sworn to win or die; and they conquered each obstacle in turn, and finally arrived before the castle, where they thrashed Ravana in several well-fought battles, in which Annouma was always in the thickest of the fight, and drove him into his citadel, — his last resort. The siege lasted ten years, with varying fortune; and before it was over, all the gods and goddesses had taken sides, — some for Rama and some for Ravana, — and were helping their favorites with every means

in their power.   At last Ravana was slain in single combat by
his adversary, and Sita was restored to her husband's arms, and
the King of Militta punished for his refusal to help him.   In
leaving Ceylon, Rama placed a giant ally on the throne, promis-

OFFERING THE BEST FRUITS OF THE LAND.

ing him that it should be his while Annouma and his race should
be honored and respected : and that this should be "as long as
the world remains held in space by the hand of its god ; as long
as the sun-god hurls his radiant darts through the ether, and the

wind-god whistles from north to south and from east to west, carrying the clouds on their errands; as long as the stars shine in the heavens, and the rising and falling sea makes a line of foam round the earth, and the lotus flower, like the spirit of creation, floats thereon. Curses upon him who fails in his worship of you, or in offering you the best fruits of his land, as he would to any god. Curses upon him who shall despise or maltreat you; for I, Rama, incarnation of Vishnu, pronounce you and your offspring sacred upon the earth, even until the ages shall bring again the return of Brahma and the last day for gods and men and every living thing."

The worship of Annouma has spread through the whole of India, and, although the followers of Vishnu especially reverence him, no sect refuses to honor him with offerings of fruit and flesh. Where these sacred apes are most common, the poor natives not only let them help themselves to anything in the garden, but actually prepare great platters of sweetened rice, which they carry piously to some one of their favorite haunts. Perhaps no people show a stranger form and object of worship than they, nor one more difficult of explanation. I once said to a Brahman with whom I was on terms of the greatest frankness, which allowed the remark, —

"You are far too intelligent to believe this story of Rama and Annouma."

"They are stories for children," he replied.

"Then how do you explain the universal credence given them?"

"I CANNOT AFFORD TO SUPPORT THEM," HE SAID.

" Simply that they have been invented to explain a feeling of indebtedness to the apes that owes its origin to their having given warning by their cries of an

MACAQUE APES.

approaching tidal wave and flood. and thereby saving whole communities, who heeded them and fled to the hill-tops."

"And how do you, who own farms and gardens, treat them when they come to devastate them?"

Smilingly he replied. " I cannot afford to support them, and so drive them off with a stick, — but I have to do it myself and at night."

During the great war in Ceylon, the warrior apes of Annouma are reported to have taken, as servants and camp followers. numerous macaques, which differ in several ways from their reputed masters. Their most interesting characteristic is their imitativeness, and it is unwise to do anything in their presence that you are unwilling they should repeat. I saw one of them imitate his mistress, whom he had watched plucking and boiling fowls, by pulling out the feathers of a pet paroquet, in spite of the latter's beak and claws, and putting him alive into the teakettle, where he was afterward found by the cook !

# CHAPTER VIII.



**T**HURSDAY and I returned to Africa laden with the spoils of our hunting trips in Borneo, and he, at least, well pleased to find himself once more in the African jungle. One night, as we were returning to camp from a hard tramp after a gorilla through swamp and forest, my guide, himself so weary that he leaned upon his bow, using it like a cane, stopped short, and motioned me to do the same.

" Listen," said he.

I could hear the distant calls of jackals and the usual thousand noises of forest life, but nothing else, and I felt that he must hear something that my duller ears could not. After a few moments of silence, during which Thursday's face expressed a growing astonishment, he condescended to explain.

" There are a number of elephants in front of us, — in fact, a whole kraal."

*Kraal* means " village " and, by wider usage, " tribe."

" How can you tell?  I hear nothing."

" But I hear their cries.  Let us advance quietly so as not to attract their attention."

I followed his advice, literally hardly breathing, although for several minutes I could distinguish nothing to suggest the presence of the huge animal. Then, however, at last I detected the curious note which characterizes them, and which grew more distinct as we moved forward toward a large clearing, filled with the bones and tusks of elephants, and from which arose a horrible stench as from decaying flesh.

"What place is this?" I asked the guide.

"An elephants' burial-place," he answered mysteriously in a whisper. "Hist! Look!" The cries redoubled. "They are bringing one of their number to the charnel-house." They were no longer *cries*, but prolonged and plaintive shrieks and howls at unequal intervals, reverberating through the forest. We hid in a ditch, and this is the strange sight we saw.

A dozen elephants suddenly appeared at the other side of the clearing, surrounding and supporting an enormous patriarch enfeebled with age and sickness. To hasten his tottering steps, they all belabored him with their trunks, urging him forward to the tomb of his ancestors, among whose bleaching bones he was coming to lay his own. The convoy having supported him to a convenient spot, stood one side, and over he went upon his side with a mournful cry that startled the birds and monkeys from the neighboring trees, and drove them, a noisy band, farther into the forest to join the jackals, whose impatience could hardly brook any delay in the giant's death, and were already hungry for his carcass. Just as the elephants were retiring into the dusky edges of the woods, Thursday made a movement that attracted their attention, and

SEARCHING FOR ELEPHANTS' TUSKS IN THEIR BURIAL-PLACES.

they turned and charged upon us! The African was brave enough when his game was caught in a pitfall. and all he had to do was to shoot poisoned arrows into his defenceless body ; but twelve active elephants on the aggressive was a different story, and he turned tail and ran for his life.

All I could think of, left in this predicament, was to fire at the leader and climb a tree.  I had no sooner done the former, than, wheeling quickly, the troop made off into the jungle at right angles to where they had come in:  When he saw that the danger was over, Thursday returned in a most penitent state of mind, and tried to make me believe that he had fled out of consideration for me, as, if the elephants had recognized him — their greatest dread — nothing could have stopped them!  On our way into camp, Thursday assured me that all communities of elephants have their burial-place, and if one of their number dies suddenly, they drag him thither that his huge carcass may not infect their haunts.  He was full of stories, and interesting ones, that would fill a volume, about this royal beast ; and I am very glad to have the opportunity to say a few words that may do some justice to this much-maligned brute, who should, much more than the lion, be called the king of beasts.

There is no living creature, even man himself aided by all the devices of civilization, that can force an elephant to do anything contrary to his wish ; nor is there cage, nor prison, nor fetter, that will hold him without his consent.  Man can kill him with the weapons of warfare, but can never tame him, like other animals, by starvation and hard treatment, but simply by an exercise of reason. ·

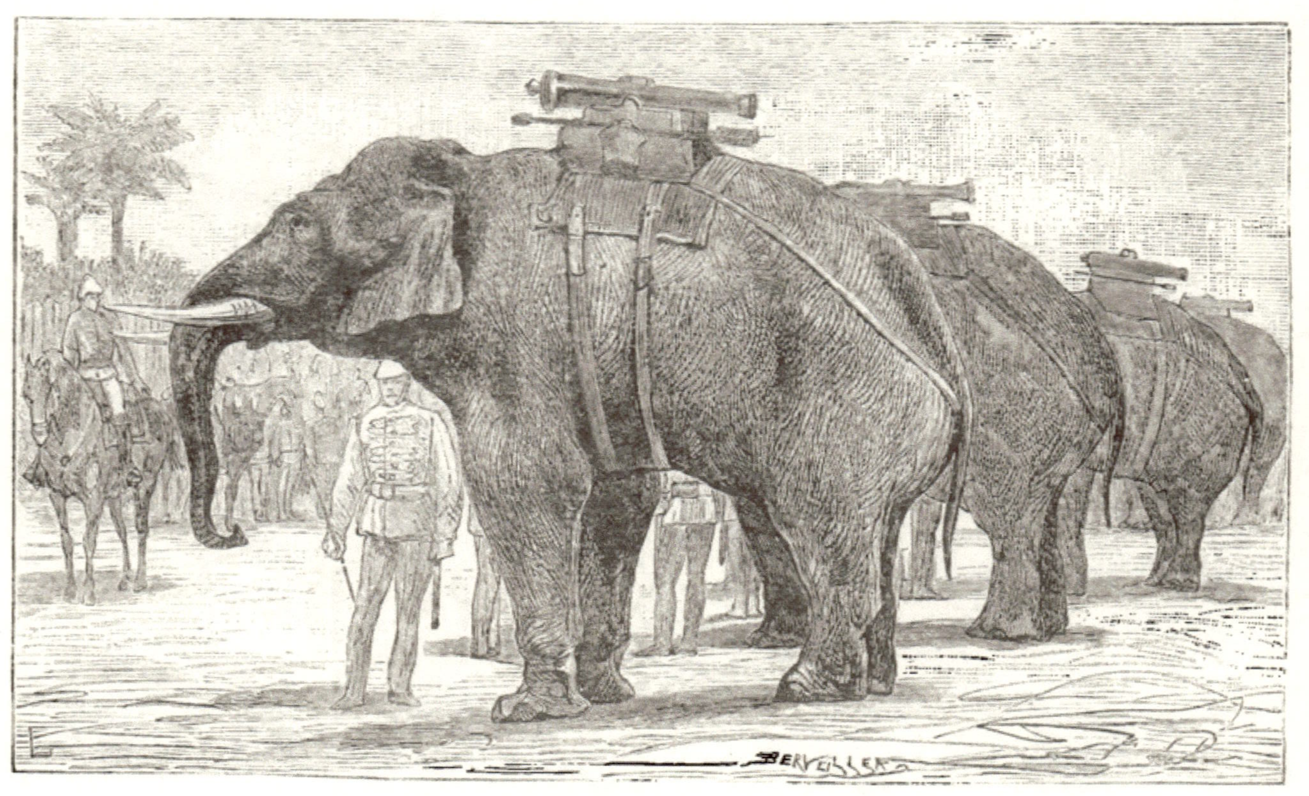

ELEPHANTS IMPRESSED INTO THE ENGLISH SERVICE.

The elephant, when once domesticated, no longer thinks of the jungles where he grew up, nor does he have moments of fury when all his savage nature returns to him. If left unconfined he does not spring upon his keeper, slay him, and escape to the wilderness, like most wild beasts; for man attracts him, and he becomes his faithful friend and the sharer of his labors. I have seen him in Ceylon; on the long roads, deep in dust, of Hindostan; in the market-places of Benares; in the jungles of Burmah and Indo-China; in the vast wildernesses of Southern Africa; and everywhere I have found him better than the men who use him, asking only, in return for his strength and his kind willingness, a little affection and good treatment. There is only one thing to be afraid of in him, and that is a madness very like that to which the human brain is subject. In this rare case he knows neither himself nor others, and, as one can do nothing with him forcibly, it is often necessary to shoot him. Sometimes this madness displays itself in an intense depression of spirits, when the elephant retires to some corner of his quarters, and refuses all food until he dies — as the natives say — of a broken heart.

This remarkable animal remembers, understands, reasons, associates ideas, and even accomplishes two of the mental processes — comparison and judgment — which are at the root of intelligence; so that, whether in point of animal or of intellectual strength, the lion makes little show before such an adversary. Indeed, his courage is nothing but unreasoning ferocity, and his generosity only a fable of certain naturalists, while his intelligence is far below that of the panther and tiger. The elephant, on the other hand, comes nearest man in point of intellect, as do the anthropoid apes in point of physical qualities.

Elephants live in communities, under chiefs to whom strict obedience is observed, and in accordance with recognized laws. The labor of obtaining food is shared among them systematically, and fruits and roots are collected for the young, their mothers, and the weak and old in regular order.

It has been urged against these animals as a proof of lack of intelligence, that the mother cannot recognize, in a herd, her own offspring from among the young of others, for they are brought up together. I am confident, from much observation, that this is not so, and that it is simply their custom to nurse any young elephant of the herd *if* their own are satisfied. Take a child five or six hours old away from its mother, and ask her, a few days later, to pick it out of a roomful of children of the same age. It does not prove, because she cannot, that she is unintelligent.

At any alarm of danger the chiefs utter a signal, easily remembered. Immediately the younger ones, guided by the females, place themselves together in the centre, with the females around them, and the males outside them. In this form they meet the attacks

of their enemies, or of others of their own race.  In the
latter case the struggle is terrific, and the forest resounds with the cries of the wounded, while the trees

ADVANCE GUARDS, LIKE SENTINELS.

bend like reeds in the wind.  Any of the conquered
males left alive take flight, and the victors adopt
children and wives of the vanquished in good old
heathen fashion.

Punishment is administered by the chiefs for acts of insubordination; and it is not uncommon to see an offender seized by older elephants. and dealt resounding blows from their trunks. When they are on the march. changing their locality, they camp each night in the form of the hollow square I have described. posting. beside, advance guards, like sentinels, to watch that no enemy steal upon them unaware.

Ever since Thursday had entered my service he had continually urged me to go on a hunt especially for elephants. assuring me that it was the most exciting and interesting sport possible. One night soon after this last adventure, he was speaking again on the same subject, and I at length consented. on one condition, — that having enjoyed all the excitement of the chase, we should not kill the elephant. Even Thursday's greed for pay. and consequent rum, would not have accepted this condition had I not promised him double wages for the whole time we were out. This brought him to terms; and he proceeded to hire four other natives as his assistants. and one fine morning we set out for elephant-land.

The five negroes were armed with shovel and pick, for we were simply going to hunt our game in ambuscade, — that is. take an elephant by tempting him into a pit covered over with branches and leaves. To make the pit. and cover it so that the elephant would not notice it. was easy enough: but what I was more anxious to see was how they would attract the game away from his herd, and draw him into the trap. We were fully sixty leagues from the coast, and all around us stretched an unbroken forest, where both good feeding-places and cool shadows, which the elephant loves, promised plenty of sport. Thursday felt confident that the very herd from which he had obtained ivory a year or more before would still have remained in such a favorable locality, where there was everything to tempt them to a long stay. That night we camped on the edge of the forest, and were careful to make as little noise as possible, and even went without a fire for cooking, to avoid any smoke that might warn the herd of our approach. We supped on maize and cassava cakes, made the day before by Thursday's wife, and on canned sardines, which I shared with my men, to their intense delight. Indeed, there is no surer passport to the hearts or greed of the blacks than a tin box of these oily fish, and they have often stood me in good stead among unfriendly natives.

If we had been scented by the elephants, they would either have attacked us or left the country for several days; for although they fear neither animal nor man, still, the latter has an entirely different effect on them from the most savage of the former. When, for instance, he suspects the presence of his deadly foe, the rhinoceros, he shakes with rage, and hastens to meet the enemy in a combat from which he almost always comes out victor: but if man approaches him he retires, if possible, into the deepest solitudes of the woods. unless he once *sees* him, when he charges upon him furiously. So it was important to take all precautions that he should not guess our presence; and we therefore, as I said. went without fire, which in Africa, surrounded as you are with wild animals. is very dangerous. Thursday chose our camp wisely. in a little half-clearing where we could see in all directions a dozen yards around us. so as to avoid surprises, and away from the river we had been following. that we might not interfere with the drinking-place of any lions or panthers in the neighborhood. My hammock was swung on a tamarind branch at a dizzy height. and I had to reach it by an athletic exhibition worthy of a chimpanzee. Fifteen feet raised me from the clutches of prowling beasts, but laid me open to the danger of breaking a limb if my sleep were at all uneasy. so with a bit of line I laced myself in. and lay secure, but sleepless. What nights these African days bring! Through the pathless forest roam wild beasts in search of food, ready to follow the first scent that promises them their prey; ravenous — except on those rare days when they have run across a buffalo strayed from his herd — and quick to take advantage of any unwary wanderer. Lions. panthers, elephants. and gorillas are here, and before the terror of their coming fly all the smaller game of the forest around.

THE ELEPHANTS' BURIAL-PLACE.

Thursday had not been mistaken in his locality, for several times during the night we heard elephants trumpeting in the neighborhood. At dawn he began his trap, — that is, he and his men set out to clean and rebuild one he had made and used the year before, — and in two hours it was done and cleverly covered in. We then, from a perch in a neighboring tree, saw him and one of his men disappear into the forest; and I was left with his wife and the other men, who could none of them understand a word of my language, nor I of theirs.

After several hours of uncomfortable waiting and listening, I heard, evidently coming toward us, the distressed cry of a young elephant and, farther off, the answering calls of his friends in the herd. Five minutes later the sounds were repeated, nearer still; and soon I saw, to my intense surprise, that the first cry proceeded from Thursday, who made use of a reed to alter the pitch of his voice, and that he was certainly drawing on after him a male and female, in search of their supposed offspring. Thursday soon joined us in the tree, and, in reply to my compliments on his powers of imitation, said *that* was easy enough, but that the difficulty lay later when the elephants were near, looking for their young one.

" Why, how is that ? "

" You see, then I must change the note to one of joy, as if he were pleased at the approach of help, for the elephant is bright enough to know that his young would not continue distressed when he saw his family coming:

and," added he, with conscious pride. "there are not three men in the business beside myself who can do this." He turned and addressed a word or two of caution to the natives, and the silence was unbroken afterward, save by the calls and answers from the elephants at intervals of a few minutes. the latter rapidly approaching our tree. At last we began to hear them breaking their way through the foliage. with occasional pauses to place the direction. evidently. from which Thursday's cries proceeded. It was one of those black nights when the darkness is so intense it seems as though daylight could never pierce it again ; and this and my strange surroundings — clinging to a tree with a handful of savages. in the midst of an almost untracked wilderness. filled with wild beasts of which so royal an example was now nearing us — gave me, for a moment. a sensation of dizziness that proved Thursday's wisdom in lashing us to the branch. Suddenly the elephant's steps ceased. and two of my guide's best-feigned cries of distress remained unanswered. I began to fear lest our scent should have reached the game. I could hear the uneven. restless breathing that indicated disquietude ; and Thursday. too. evidently thought it time to change his tactics. for he uttered a much shriller and longer cry than before. to which the elephant replied by a soft and more agreeable note. almost like a mother's call.

"It is a female," whispered Thursday. rapidly. and, without waiting for reply. he continued his quicker cries, with a climax of great distress, as if the little elephant had suddenly. been the victim of some fresh violence. To each reply he had a new note, pitched to marvellous

"IT IS A FEMALE," WHISPERED THURSDAY.

agreement with the female's mood. His last call ended our long waiting; for, with a threatening note, the huge animal charged forward to the rescue, breaking down all obstacles *en route*, until *crash* she went into the pitfall.

"We have her," shouted Thursday, and with his native friends, began indulging in expressions of extravagant delight. It would have broken your heart to hear her piteous notes when these unaccustomed sounds reached her, trapped through her love for her young, and, in spite of frantic efforts, unable to get out of Thursday's cleverly arranged trap. The latter was ungenerous enough to utter again some of the cries of distress that had first deceived her, until I ordered him sharply to desist. Pity for a vanquished enemy is something that never enters a negro's head, and sympathy with a wounded or suffering animal strikes him as superlatively ridiculous, and I was compelled to repeat my order angrily to obtain obedience.

The rest of the night passed in comparative quiet, although the elephant never ceased to struggle to escape; and my conscience reproached me that I should have been the cause of sacrificing her to her maternal instincts. As dawn came her struggles seemed to cease, for we no longer heard her frantic movements, which, we inferred, had wearied her. Thursday and I climbed down, when it was light, and approached our captive. What was our astonishment to see her, with the aid of her tusks, digging into the bank and trampling down the earth to aid her escape! This accounted for the silence of the last few hours, and had we given her a few more she would have succeeded easily. The animal was so intent on her work that she did not at first notice us, but when she did, she associated us at once with her misfortunes, and began to utter terrible cries, waving her trunk back and forth as if to threaten us.

"Don't go too near." Thursday cautioned me. "See!"

As he spoke he held out toward the angry beast a bamboo rod, which she grasped, almost dragging him with it, and broke into a thousand pieces, which she threw back at us with greater force than accuracy. This was followed by small stones and lumps of earth, her fury seeming to increase each moment, and her cries growing louder and more penetrating.

"We shall have the whole herd down upon us, if this goes on," muttered my guide, and, as if to confirm his statement, the distant trumpetings of many elephants could be heard answering their companion. Evidently the safest thing to do was to retreat as quickly as possible; but we had hardly reached our tree of refuge before the advance guard appeared on the edge of the clearing, and behind, hundreds of trunks and mighty heads were visible among the branches; the former like great serpents in motion, winding round and uprooting any trees in the way of the herd's advance. It was a terrible and inspiring sight to see this army of faithful friends hurrying to the assistance of their comrade, whose cries were now of joy. In an instant two of the animals laid hold upon her and freed her from the pit, and surrounding her, the herd testified to their joy at finding her, in almost human caresses. All this lasted but a few moments, and they turned for revenge upon those who had invaded their solitude.　With unerring accuracy in placing us and our refuge, they surrounded the tree and menaced

us with upraised trunks, while cries of fury resounded through the forest.

Fortunately the tree in which we were sheltered was a safe refuge from any attack, on account of its enormous size and strength. From one of these gigantic trunks, as a parent centre, the banyan reaches out its arms, that droop until they touch the ground, take root, and add new trees to the old. In this way I have seen a whole forest grow from three or four banyan trunks, enlarging on the circumference, until the circle reaches some insurmountable obstacle like a lake, or river, or sandy waste. And so this banyan that we were in had its offshoots in all directions, and some twenty of them in the immediate neighborhood almost as large as itself. The elephants soon recognized their impotence in reaching us, and at a call from their leader, drew off to consult. That they can communicate their ideas is certain, and was again proved in this case, for after a time most of the herd calmly turned their backs and started for the same woods from which they had come.

"We are saved!" shouted I, joyfully.

"Not yet, Sahib."

"What do you mean? They are giving it up."

"But they leave eight guards to prison us here, until we drop, from hunger and exhaustion, into their clutches! We are likely to end our days here."

A shiver ran down my back as I saw his prophecy fulfilled by eight great animals still lingering around the tree, feeding on the clumps of fresh pasture and green buds from the branches. Every now and then they came nearer, and raising their trunks in anger tried to reach us where we sat, and coming high enough to fan us with their hot breath.

"Come. Thursday," said I, "you cannot have been so skilful a hunter all these years without having found some way out of this predicament, in which you must have been placed before."

I saw my man was thoroughly frightened, and I resolved to try this flattery on him; it produced a favorable effect, although he replied sadly enough,—

"Yes, once. I took refuge in a similar tree to the one we are now in."

"Well?"

"Well, the elephants, as now, placed sentinels, and I remained three days without food or drink, until I could hardly hold on to my branch. My wife, luckily, had been able to escape the first night of our captivity, and she ran by forced stages to the nearest village of our tribe. All the warriors armed themselves and came to the rescue."

"You mean to say that they dare to fight the elephant at close quarters?"

"Oh, no! They came several thousand strong, shouting, beating the tam-tam, and making a tremendous noise, for that is what the elephant dislikes, and off they went."

"And does not your experience suggest any means of escape?"

After reflecting, he replied,—

THE HERD CALMLY TURNED THEIR BACKS AND STARTED FOR THE WOODS.

"Yes, there are two,—but both dangerous. We might set fire to the forest and dry underbrush around us. The trees would burn last, and there would be a chance — perhaps one in ten — of our escaping alive, as the elephants would be driven off immediately by the burning undergrowth."

"But how would you set the fire, when we cannot leave this branch?"

"By lighting my cotton drawers, and throwing them down among those dry leaves there!" he replied with a triumphant smile.

"Well," said I, laughing at the fellow's ingenuity, and glad to see his confidence returning. "if your second idea is less practicable, we will try this one. But let's hear it."

Just as he started to tell me, one of the elephants came nearer the tree, and standing close beside it, watching us with angry eyes, he raised his flexible trunk as far as he could, trying to reach us. His hot breath fanned us violently, and it gave me a dizzy feeling to see within how few feet he came of his prey. Seeing his inability to quite reach us, the animal uttered the most terrible noises, and his companions joined him in the assault, hurling their ponderous bodies against the tree, and shaking us as if it were a sapling. One of the elephants raised himself so high that he lost his balance and went over with a crash; before he could recover himself, one of the others stepped upon his huge side, as if it were a hassock, and his trunk waved in our very faces. Thursday and I, instinctively, had thrown ourselves back, or one of us would have been taken and crushed. Quick as thought, Thursday buried his lance in the enemy's trunk, and the elephant dropped upon the ground uttering piercing cries of pain.

"How foolish of you!" I cried: "you will only add to their fury."

"You are mistaken, massa. Thursday is not foolish. The intelligent animals, having discovered by accident the way to reach our place of refuge, would in five minutes all be making use of this means, and we should be driven higher, to a less comfortable spot."

He was evidently right, for though the wound he had inflicted could hardly have been deep, still, this one of our sentinels departed into the forest, whining like a whipped child. For the elephant, in spite of his great mass and thick hide, is very sensitive to physical pain when his blood is not up in a fight.

"Now we have only seven guards," said I, triumphantly. "If we could only get rid of them all in the same way!"

"Don't be too sure, massa; the substitute for this one will not be long in putting in an appearance."

"Do you think so?"

"I am sure of it. I know these animals only too well."

"Then let us hear your alternative method of escape."

"Its danger lies in our number. Were you and I alone, we might easily make use of it. You see these almost horizontal branches, running off to the different tree trunks?"

"Yes. Well?"

"Well, at night we might, if alone, creep silently along these, holding our breath, until we reached the nearest clearing, perhaps a hundred yards away, and then drop to the ground and run for our lives."

"That does not sound very difficult. What is your objection to it?"

"Because, although he does not see at night so well as the lion or the tiger, still, the elephant discerns objects well enough to guide himself in the dark, and his hearing is very acute; so that at the least noise on our part, the guards would follow us from tree to tree to crush us when we dropped to their reach."

"Never mind, this is our only chance, and we must try it to-night, before we grow weak from lack of food."

"All right, but it will be wise to separate in couples. I will take you first, then my wife and child, and the two guides last, by themselves."

"Wouldn't it be a good idea for those left behind to make as much noise as possible, to draw the attention of the elephants, and cover our retreat?"

"Yes, and I should not have thought of it," acknowledged my guide; "it will double our chances."

"Then you think there *is* a chance?"

" Yes, for the first at least ; and I am at your orders."

At this instant we heard a distant trumpeting.

"Here comes the substitute for the wounded elephant," said Thursday.

" Are you sure ? "

" Look ! "

A hundred yards away a black mass bent aside the tall plants and young trees in its way, disdaining to uproot them.  It was really an elephant ; and although at first I could hardly believe he came in place of his wounded companion. I saw from his reception that he was an old acquaintance. and, after greetings like those I have before mentioned. he went quietly to his station " on guard."   The lesson. however. had been learned, and the elephants tried no further assault on our citadel.

At the foot of our tree, exactly under us, lay a provision box containing the food we had brought for breakfast after the hunt, which in our sudden retreat we had forgotten to take with us.  We should have been glad to have it at this moment. for as the sun rose higher in the heavens, our hunger grew upon us ; and so tantalizingly near were some two pounds of pilot bread, several boxes of canned meats, and half-a-dozen bottles of wine and rum.

" How *can* we get that box ? " said I to Thursday for the tenth time.  " We can't go all day without food."

" It is almost impossible to get it up here. but it might be done."

"I'll give you a bottle of rum if you can." Thursday's eyes sparkled at the mere thought, as he answered, "I will drop to the ground, and before the elephants

LOOK !

can reach the tree from where they are now grazing, will fasten my girdle to the box, so that you can draw it up, and get back again in safety."

"You would do better to have one of your companions go."

"No, I want all the rum for myself."

"As you like."

While he was speaking he began to unwind the coco fibre girdle that he wore, and handed it to me, watching our captors grazing at a little distance. I tied a slip noose in the other end, and the two natives stood ready to heave on the line when it should be attached to the coveted prize. Success seemed possible, though uncertain, as he gently slid down the trunk, on the side farthest from the enemy. I stood breathless, watching the latter, and ready to give the signal that his movements were noticed. Everything went well until he touched the ground, when the whole herd caught sight of him simultaneously, and charged upon him with surprising speed.

"Back, quick!" I shouted, "or you are lost!"

Without listening to my caution he reached the box at a bound, raised it, passed the cord around it, and the natives drew it up in an instant. Then the guide turned to escape, but too late! The furious brutes were not ten paces from him, and would have pulled him down had he started to ascend. He was lost! We shouted and yelled to distract the elephants' attention, and the woman and her child uttered heart-rending screams, but in vain.

The African stood firm, his back against the tree, without arms, awaiting his fate. He had not an instant to live, when — shall I ever forget it? — with an agility and strength that were marvellous, he sprang between the approaching giants, and in a dozen bounds was at the foot of one of the auxiliary trunks of our banyan and half way up it!

He had counted upon the difficulty these huge bodies have in turning quickly, and not in vain, for their very number impeded them; and as they tried to turn, closely packed together, they gave Thursday the few seconds necessary to make good his escape, and rejoin us who had given him up as lost.

This exploit raised my guide immensely in my opinion, for he had shown address, coolness, and strength such as few men possess, and I could not help pressing his hand with real emotion, as he stood once more beside me.

"I hope I have earned my rum," was his first very practical thought and speech!

I handed it to him, and presented the rest of the party also with a bottle to drink his health. The result of the adventure was that the elephants never left us the rest of the day, and that we made a hearty breakfast that raised our spirits beyond caring for them or their anger, — such is the close relation between the stomach and courage. As the natives finished their rum, they hurled the bottles down on the elephants with all kinds of curses and taunts. It seemed as though the day would never end. But at last the sun began its downward course, and we took rapid counsel in regard to our attempted escape. When the moment arrived Thursday said simply, —

"Give me your rifle, that you may be unincumbered, and follow me."

Although I had observed with care the route over which I knew we were to go, still, at night, I found I was helpless except as Thursday led me like a child.

Our companions began to sing and clap their hands to drown any sound of our movements, and, as it was black as Egypt, not even an owl could have seen us. The noise was infernal, and the elephants replied with heavy, deep grunts.

I seized the branch, and began to crawl along it as quietly as I could behind my guide. With the woodsman's instinct he assisted me from tree to tree five times, and then we rested to see if we had been followed. You never heard such a racket as those negroes kept up, but we felt confident from the elephants' replies that they had not yet suspected our absence, and we renewed our line of march over branches growing slighter and slighter, until we felt that safety demanded our quitting them for firmer footing. As we dropped to the ground, we knew from the fainter sounds that we were at quite a respectable distance from our starting-point, even should the elephants undertake to follow us. Cautiously we threaded the dense forest, in darkness so complete I could hardly see the indistinct outline of my guide two paces ahead of me. After an hour's march we came at last to the edge

I SEIZED THE BRANCH, AND BEGAN TO CRAWL ALONG IT.

of the forest and might reasonably consider ourselves out of danger. Thursday assured me of this joyful fact, adding, —

"And now I must return."

"And leave me?"

"Thursday must go back after his wife and child."

"True; I had forgotten. And I?"

"Travel straight toward the south, keeping that star always on your left hand, and at daybreak you will reach the stream we crossed yesterday and have nothing further to fear from wild beasts. It will then, and not till then, be safe to sleep."

"All right."

"I will join you at our last camp with everything left behind us in the jungle."

"I shall not soon forget your devotion to my interests, Thursday, and — "

My guide grasped my arm and drew me behind a bush.

"I heard a twig snap," whispered he. "We are followed!"

"By elephants?"

"Oh, no; we should hear *them* fast enough, without any difficulty." As he said this he imitated the note of a bird, clear and delicious. The same note was echoed by a voice not far distant, and in a moment we had the very welcome sight of Thursday's wife and boy coming out of the trees' shadow and approaching us. This, of course, altered our plans; and we took up our march in single file toward camp, well pleased at our fortunate escape from this dangerous locality, where we had seen the African elephant in his most terrible mood.

The two natives also got off scot-free, and reported later at camp, where we celebrated our escape by the best feast our supplies afforded.

# CHAPTER IX.



A FEW ELEPHANT STORIES.

E have seen one side of the elephant's nature in his wild state, but it is only fair to remember his gentleness and friendliness in captivity, which is really voluntary, because he might with a blow of his trunk annihilate his keepers and escape to his native jungle. In his long life he often changes his master, but his allegiance goes too; and he is devoted to each, and figures alike as porter, wood-cutter, errand-boy, hunter, gladiator in fights with tigers, and artillery-man.

I have seen, in India, elephants let out by their owners as choppers, working like day-laborers and returning at night to sleep at home, — that is, at their master's. These intelligent animals, armed with long axes, the use of which they have been taught, cut, at otherwise perfectly impracticable heights, the gigantic trees which are used in the keels of vessels, carry them to the nearest port, and deliver them to other elephants to pile, — a feat which they accomplish with the greatest regularity and with a strength that no number of men can equal. They work alone, too, without any special oversight on the part of the keeper, who often comes but once a day to note their progress; and yet there is not a case on record where one of them has attempted to return to his free life in the forest. or rejoin his former companions enjoying themselves in the neighboring ravines, while he is working hard on the hills above. Indeed, they grow to hate their untamed cousins, and fight them — and usually successfully — at every opportunity, bearing them away in bondage to their masters.

The English have made use of their enormous strength in all the wars in India and. more recently, in Africa, where without them the troops would have been helpless to move the artillery, even the lighter pieces, which these dumb allies carried bravely into action on their backs, while their courage under fire has been attested by special mention in reports from the English officers. One of them says : —

"In our marches across Bengal we used elephants in the baggage train. so well disposed to us that, without waiting for a command from the keeper, if a wagon stuck, one of them would hurry up, put his mighty shoulder to the wheel, and never rest till it was rolling on smoothly again. Then he would return to his own proper place and duty in the line again. One morning. in the press of wagons and animals, one of the elephants was hurt by the heavy wheel of a cart running over his foot. I happened to be near. and bound it up with a towel dipped in camphorated brandy. and tightened the bandage as well as I could. and off he limped to his stable. In the afternoon I went to

PILING THEM WITH THE GREATEST REGULARITY.

see how he was getting on. He was lying on a bed of
straw; he recognized me at once, and held out his wounded
foot for me to see. I renewed the bandage each day; and

HE HELD OUT HIS WOUNDED FOOT FOR ME TO SEE.

after that the grateful animal never passed my tent without a peculiar cry which he used for that occasion alone,
and when he met me he always gently rubbed my back

or shoulders with his trunk, uttering little sniffs of pleasure."

Major Skinner, of the English Army, vouches for the following story, which shows on the part of the elephant intelligence, memory, comparison, judgment, and good-nature.

Riding along a very narrow trail near Kandy, in Ceylon, where he happened to be stationed, he heard the heavy tread of an approaching elephant, uttering discontented grunts which frightened his rather nervous horse, and made him rear and plunge. He says:—

"I soon saw whence these sounds proceeded. A tame elephant had undertaken the difficult task of transporting a long girder, resting on his tusks, over the narrow road. Between the trees on either side there was not room for this to pass, and he could only advance by turning his head from side to side and avoiding each tree as he went. It was a slow business, and no wonder he complained; but on seeing how his trumpetings frightened my horse, he ceased instantly, threw down his load, and pressed his huge body close up against the trees on one side of the road to allow us to pass. My horse trembled all over, and refused to move, seeing which, the elephant drew still farther back and tried to encourage the coward by a gentler note.

"Finally the latter plucked up enough heart to dash by on his way, when the faithful elephant resumed the laborious errand in which we had found him engaged.

" This elephant had, before the campaign, been used as a watchman by his owner, whose estates bordered on a river. Marauders would drop down the stream in their craft, and rob the gardens and orchards, and be off again without leaving any other trace of their coming than the empty trees and ravaged beds. Tired of losing the fruits of his labor, the owner had trained this elephant to perform sentinel duty along the bank; and, when danger threatened, the animal would growl like a dog, and filling his huge trunk with water from the stream, would play upon the rascals like a fire-engine, drowning them out of their boat like rats. until they were glad to hoist sail and make off to the best of their ability."

The art of hunting the elephant, although of most ancient origin, is practised to-day on a larger scale than ever before, because of the services which the English have found he can perform for them. As long as elephants were used simply to add splendor to the suite of a rajah, or dignity to one of the religious processions, it sufficed to hunt single animals, capturing them by a decoy elephant ridden by a native. who provoked and held the attention of the game, while another ran up behind and cleverly passed a chain around one of his legs. Bound in this way the elephant was sure. under the influence of starvation, and the example of his former companions, to yield eventually to his captors. Now the country is divided into " preserves," over which

a royal officer is appointed, and immense hunting parties are made up, and whole herds captured at once:
although it is no easy thing to take alive and un-
wounded an animal that has at once such strength and
such intelligence as the elephant. It could not be done
without the aid of other elephants, who bring their
attachment to their masters to this high point, and
having assisted in the capture, go still farther and in-
struct the captives in their future duties. The trait of
obedience is, however, rather the result of affection than
fear, and in this regard the elephant's docility is more
like that of the dog than of the horse. It even leads
them to bear the pain of the worst surgical operations,
like the burning out with a hot iron of tumors or ulcers,
or the taking of the most bitter medicines at the hands
of their "approved good masters."

The only way in which the male's gentle temper can
be spoiled is by a course of special diet of certain kinds
of food: and this is the means resorted to by their less
gentle masters when they wish them to fight, — either
one another, or their feudal enemy, the tiger. In India
I was once invited by a Rajah to attend his celebration
of the Feast of Moharem, where the principal attraction
is the display of elephants. I accepted, of course.

The Feast began by a tiger fight. A space some fifty
feet square had been fenced off near the river, and we
occupied a special "box," protected, in case of accident,
by a bamboo network strong enough to keep the tiger

PLAYING UPON THEM LIKE A FIRE-ENGINE.

out should the fancy strike him to turn to us for sport. He was loosed into the arena, around which he circled several times, and at last stopped directly in front of us and stood looking at us in a way that made me bless the foresight that had built the screen. But immediately a buffalo was driven into the circle, and advanced slowly toward the crouching tiger, who was ready for a spring. Seeing this he stopped short. his horns low, snorting with anger. But the tiger paid no attention to him, nor to five more buffaloes which were let loose one after the other, treating them with sublime disdain, as foemen unworthy of his steel. A curious incident happened just then: a small dog fell into the arena from one of the seats, and toward him with stately steps the tiger stalked, without, however, any appearance of anger. The dog, frightened, ran whining round the edge of the enclosure, and after him the tiger, faster and faster. Finally, seeing he could not escape, and that one or two more leaps would be his last. he turned and with real *grit* showed his teeth to his pursuer. We supposed he would be crushed at a blow; but not at all. At the instant the tiger was about to spring upon him, the brute seemed to change his mind, and, like a cat after a mouse, crouched watching and playing with him. Then the Nabob ordered them to let in the elephant.

The crowd were hushed in silence. Either the tiger must fight or be killed ingloriously. A gate opened, and

the elephant. his keeper on his back, advanced into the
arena. At the sight of the huge animal the tiger uttered
a long howl, which was most evidently one of terror.
for he sprang against the palisade several times. and
did his best to break it down and escape. At sight of
him the elephant became madly excited. and made
straight at him. blocking his wild efforts at flight.
and almost trampling him under foot. before he realized that fight was the only alternative. Then, and
only then. he sprang upon the head of his adversary
and endeavored to maintain his hold with claws and
teeth. But the elephant wound his enormous trunk
around the tiger's body. lifted him in the air, and hurled
him, bruised and broken. down upon the ground twenty
feet away. The tiger was half dead, and wholly helpless, and lay where he fell in a stupor. This exploit
accomplished, the victor did not deign to push his
triumph farther. but turned and saluted the Nabob in
our box as respectfully as would a slave, and peaceably
departed through the door by which he had entered.
without paying any attention to the applause and cheers
that followed him.

The remaining festivities were then postponed until
the next day, when. after breakfast in the garden of the
Nabob, we adjourned to a tent on the river-bank at a
favorite bathing-place of the elephants, where we were
to see a fight between two of the largest of them. The
plain was covered with a dense crowd of people, and a

regiment of soldiers and a squad of cavalry had been ordered out to do us honor. and hold the crowd back. The interpreter explained to us that it was not properly

HE SPRANG UPON HIS ADVERSARY'S HEAD AND HELD WITH CLAWS AND TEETH

a fight that we were about to witness. but rather a joust. in which the combatants would not try to injure each other seriously, but simply display their strength and skill. The two elephants were led in by their native keepers, and were by all odds the finest specimens I had ever seen. Of unusual size, with black, shining coats, eyes full of fire, tusks long and perfect, they advanced with an air of assurance that promised a tremendous struggle. At first they approached each other at a rapid pace until within a few feet, when they stopped and, at the command of their riders, saluted in good Marquis of Queensbury style. This done, their keepers lay down upon their respective elephant's backs, and held tightly to the girdle while the fight began.

The two elephants sprang upon each other with a shock that threw them on their hind legs, their trunks up and intertwined, swaying back and forth in, for the riders at least, a most unpleasant way. The plucky fellows clung fast, however, and encouraged their favorites with voice and hand. The tactics of the pair seemed to be to try to force the weaker, or the less adroit, backward into the river, and after an hour of intense effort and struggle, one of the elephants had so far lost ground that he was compelled to jump into the river to avoid being thrown in. This was supposed to end the combat; but his adversary insisted on following him across the river, in spite of the united efforts of the Nabob's servants and tamers. The conflict was evidently to be renewed on the other bank, where the first animal had taken a favorable position, from which for fully thirty minutes he prevented the other from landing, thrusting him back, at every attempt, into the water. The fight was declared a draw, and the prize — a load of sugar-cane, of which they are very fond — was divided between them.

There were several other combats of a like nature, in one of which the elephants indulged in spouting immense streams of water at each other, but not different in the main from the one I have described. In the evening, when the crowd had departed, we were invited to watch a curious fishing in the river, with otters. These animals, as clever as dogs, dive into the water, and, as they are taught, either drive the fish toward the nets, or help bring the latter ashore, handling the fish with their jaws without hurting them, or breaking them at all.

The whole performance, lighted up by the flaring torches, is most picturesque. On leaving him the next day, the Nabob presented me with two beautiful elephants, and upon one or the other of them I rode many miles through the jungle. Of one of these fine animals he told me an interesting story.

He was originally the property of an old Indian, rich in gold and in a young and lovely wife. The elephant was a great favorite of the latter, and, if one can use the term of so large a beast, was a family pet. Now the old Brahman died soon after his marriage, and the priests of his religion endeavored to convince his widow that she must sacrifice her life on the funeral pyre, in accordance with the dreadful practice of their church. They held up before her bright eyes the extraordinary rewards that she would receive in the next world, and the divine pleasures that awaited her in the halls of Brahma. Besides this, she had the surety of a sad life did she refuse to offer herself a willing victim to her belief; for a widow cannot remarry in India, and she lives with her own family in the greatest poverty and distress, because there is a superstition that the house is unlucky where a widow dwells, and her relatives give her barely enough to keep body and soul together. For this same reason they are nearly always as anxious to have their widowed relative burned as are the fanatic priests themselves. But in spite of the pressure brought to bear upon her, this girl refused to commit *sutty*, as it is called; and the priests were forced to use drugs in her food, under the influence of which she was induced to yield her consent. When she returned to herself she found the priests rejoicing over a consent of which she remembered nothing, and saw with horror their preparations for the funeral procession and pyre. Suddenly an idea occurred to her; and she assumed a willing and inspired air, even offering to grace the procession with her husband's stately elephants, on one of which, arrayed in her most gorgeous dress and jewels, she would ride. This pretended conversion was announced to the people as a new miracle and sign of Brahma's approval, and the young widow, from being scorned and insulted, became the heroine of the hour.

As the moment for the last ceremonies approached, she

had her favorite elephant trapped in all the splendor she could muster, decorating him with the silks and jewels she herself could not wear, and caressing his silky trunk until he whinnied with pleasure. Mounted on his back, she led the procession, followed by the corpse in the funeral palanquin and the paid mourners weeping and rending the air with mock lamentations.

Children threw flowers along the road, and nautch girls sang and danced beside it. The coolies had piled high the fiery couch, and added quantities of oil to make it burn brighter and hotter around the withered old flesh and the fresh, warm life that were to be consigned to it together. As soon as the cortége reached the pyre, the musicians began their doleful playing, and the priests came forward to receive the victim. The moment had come!

As she did not descend from her seat, the priests made a sign to the keeper, who ordered his elephant to kneel, and then offered Mariana his hand to help her down. But she declined *in toto*, clinging to the elephant's girdle and uttering the most piercing shrieks and praying my elephant to save her.

When the priests saw they had been tricked, they rushed toward Mariana furiously, fearing to lose their victim; but it was too late. The elephant seized the Brahman leading the wretches, lifted him into the air with his trunk, and dashed him down senseless. In vain the keeper called him in tones of entreaty and command. He was past control, and knew only that his beloved

mistress was in peril. Springing to his feet, he opened
a passage through the crowd with tremendous blows of
his trunk, before which one or two Brahmans fell at each

HE WAS PAST CONTROL.

stroke, crushed and injured. It became a perfect rout.
Thirty or more were killed or wounded, and many more
trodden under foot. Mariana was saved!

As soon as she reached the open country she took the road to the nearest English settlement, and my Nabob's was the first house where she rested in her flight. In gratitude for his immense kindness to her, she gave him her protector, the elephant; and he, with the faithfulness I have described, transferred his allegiance to his new master and then to me. Mariana, meanwhile, reached the district magistrate, a hundred miles farther on, in whose family she remained and with whom she returned to England. This is the only case I know, by the way, of a Brahman voluntarily going into exile.

The elephant plays an important part in other native festivals besides this one of the Moharem, and I have seen, in a sacred procession in India at the feast of Juggernaut, over two hundred of the native devotees called fakirs throw themselves down beneath the white elephants, where they were sure of being crushed under their ponderous feet.

I have already spoken of the intelligence and memory of the elephant. In Ceylon I once saw a fine herd of fifteen elephants, used by the chief magistrate as his hunting stud, lying under the spreading trees around his house, as is their custom. A sudden thunder-storm came up, with the vivid flashes and tremendous claps of thunder of that latitude; when the elephants, instead of taking refuge still closer under the trees, at the first flash moved quickly out into the open away from shelter, stood stoically through the down-pour, and as soon as the rain was over returned to the shade. I was greatly surprised, knowing how the animals disliked cold rain-water, but my friend the judge quickly enlightened me. Several years before, one of his hunting elephants had been struck by lightning while standing under a tree in the park, and ever since the herd had gone through the tactics I had observed, at the first indications of a thunder-storm, and had taught all the new-comers the same habit of safety. This faculty of communicating ideas is well established. I remember once trying to cross a stream on the back of a favorite elephant, when he and all the others in the party, but he first, absolutely refused to put foot into the water. After reasoning with him and punishing him, and all in vain, my driver grumbling all the while at the impossibility of altering his mind, I recalled that a year before at this very ford he had hurt his foot on a sharp stone in the river-bed. That he should have remembered it was very singular, but more so that he could make his companions share his fear of repeating the accident; but that both these things happened is certain, for by riding a few hundred yards down the stream to another ford, we had no difficulty in getting them to carry us over without special urging.

In the Indian colonies, especially on the coast of Malabar, where one travels days through unbroken forest and jungle meeting only wild beasts, the postal service is done by a native mounted on the most intelligent and fastest travelling elephant obtainable. Many of the stories told

OVER TWO HUNDRED NATIVE DEVOTEES THREW THEMSELVES BENEATH THE WHITE ELEPHANT'S FEET.

of these mail-carriers sound too remarkable to believe; but I remember, when the cholera was prevalent one year, that the rider mounted on one of these government

HE SET OUT AT A TREMENDOUS PACE.

despatch animals died *en route* at a miserable little village a day's journey and more from his destination. The chief of the village, recognizing from the badge on the forehead of the elephant that he was in the government service, tried to get him to accept one of his own riders in place of the dead man, but he could not accomplish it, for if any one even approached the body or the despatches he broke into uncontrollable fury, and effectually prevented any interference with them.

Seeing that his efforts were of no use, the chief let him have his own way, and simply ordered two mounted soldiers to follow him. Taking his former rider and the mail-bags across his neck, he set out at a tremendous pace for his original destination, where he arrived without stop in twelve hours, leaving the horsemen far behind, ride as they might.

Later this same faithful animal was attacked by an ophthalmia which was pronounced incurable by the English veterinary surgeons, and sold to the Brahman priests of a rich monastery near by. These skilful men cured him so quickly as to suggest the idea of a conspiracy to aid them in getting so valuable an acquisition at a low price. At any rate, they made capital use of him, sending him far and near within a radius of thirty leagues with a bag hung at his neck, into which he put everything given him, like a good mendicant friar; and what he received he knew well how to protect from all comers.

One day I saw him pumping water into the trough at which the animals belonging to the friars drank, — for this was one of his regular duties, — but in an unusually impatient way that attracted my attention to the cause. And no wonder, for some mischievous rascal had put a large

THE ELEPHANT HAD AN INSPIRATION.

log under the end of the trough, and as fast as the water flowed in at one end it flowed out at the other! He seemed greatly pleased to see me, probably thinking I

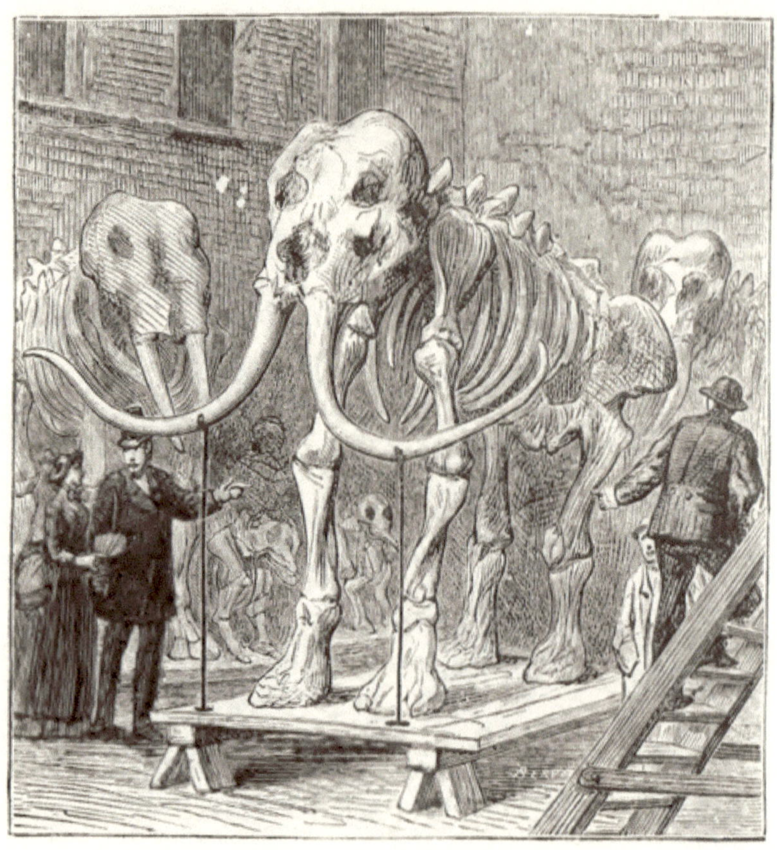

THE SKELETONS OF HIS ANCESTORS.

could solve his difficulty; but I preferred to stand by and see him get out of it as best he could by himself. After several attempts to fill the inclined trough, and an equal number of pauses for reflection and grunting, he had an inspiration. Winding his trunk around the trough at the raised end, he lifted it still higher, and with his foot pushed the log from under, replacing the trough at its proper angle in triumph and pumping it full with evident satisfaction.

Indeed, this animal only lacked speech to be quite human. The same fellow who played this unhandsome trick, from which my friend had come out with such flying colors, was always bothering the elephant, and finally this bad treatment grew to such proportions that even this gentle animal's patience came to an end. Although he might easily have killed the offender with a blow from his mighty trunk, he preferred to take revenge in practical jokes, like crowding the man into a marsh when dressed in his best, or drenching him to the skin with a torrent of muddy water spouted from the creek, or dropping him gently into the centre of a cactus-plant! His ingenuity in planning and success in executing these little annoyances were so great that the unhappy man was actually driven from the monastery, and sought employment elsewhere.

It is singular how widely distributed the elephant has been, and in how very few countries he can now be found. The skeletons of his ancestors are preserved in many of our museums, and their bones are whitening almost within the polar circle, where the whalers often find them, coated with ice, their tusks adding to the poor sailors' prize-money.

THE WHALERS OFTEN FIND THEM, COATED WITH ICE.

# CHAPTER X.

## HUNTING THE RHINOCEROS.

FTER the elephant, the rhinoceros is the largest animal on the globe; and I have followed him along the great rivers. through the marshes and dense forests of Southern Africa. India, Java. and Sumatra, where alone he is now found, although. like the elephant, he was once much more common. There are two varieties living. — one with one horn. the other with two; and it is to the latter class that the African rhinoceros belongs. His eyes are small and deep-set ; his horns — one in front of the other — are of different size and conical in shape, and not attached to the bone of the nose, but simply to the skin, which is almost hairless except at the tail, and along the ears. He lives in the most untracked solitudes. near the large rivers, and especially where a variety of acacia grows of which he is very fond. Both classes of rhinoceros are, like all vegetable-eating animals. fairly peaceable. and he never attacks without provocation; but when his blood is up he becomes blindly furious. and his strength and ferocity are without bounds. The deep grunting noise which he makes ordinarily then becomes

a shrill, piercing note, and he rushes rapidly straight
ahead, overturning every obstacle, uprooting trees,
ploughing the ground with his terrible tusks, and vent-

THE ONE-HORNED RHINOCEROS.

ing his rage on whatever he meets. Covered as he is
with a tough and little sensitive hide, he fears neither
the rifle-ball nor the claws of the tiger and lion, and
even has been said to attack the mighty elephant,

disembowelling him with his tusk at a single blow. If, however, his first attack is unsuccessful. the elephant immediately crushes him with his greater strength and weight, and kills him before he can make a second lunge.

Although of little intelligence, he is sometimes domesticated and his unreasoning strength turned to use about the farm.

The natives are very fond of rhinoceros flesh. and to obtain it, take advantage of the animal's slowness in turning, creeping silently into his lair, approaching him from behind. and, before he can turn to gore them. burying a spear in his heart. Should the blow miss its aim, the hunters. who practise this dangerous sport in couples, spring upon trained horses that they have in readiness, and are off like the wind.

The animal's enormous appetite and thirst prevents his staying long in any one spot, and only then. where the food is very abundant, as he consumes two hundred pounds a day. Besides the flesh. the horns are greatly valued by the superstitious natives, and cups made from them are supposed to render harmless any liquor they may contain, and knives and swords with horn handles are believed never to miss their man. From the heart's blood is prepared a sacred philter curing fevers, serpent bites, and wounds received in battle; while from the teeth and nails are made rosaries which protect from spirits, wizards. and even death itself. In

Siam the horns are so highly prized that the king, wishing to especially honor Louis XIV., sent him six, as the rarest treasures he possessed.

There is one point on which naturalists cannot agree in regard to him, and that is whether in Abyssinia he is really used to replace the ox in field labor. However, this much I know, that there is a vast country south of Egypt and bordering on the Nile, inhabited by an ancient race which has clung to life through all the vicissitudes that have visited this continent. Driven back, first by the invaders from the South, and then by the conquerors of Egypt, they owe their preservation to the rocky deserts among which they retired, and over the possession of which no one cared to dispute. They live between the first and second cataracts of the Nile, and have preserved many of the characteristics of the old Egyptian type. Their figures are tall and elegant, their limbs well formed, but generally slender, their coloring delicate, and the slight amount of hair upon their faces is more than compensated for by the bushy growth upon the top of their heads. This silky covering is made an even greater protection against the hot sun of their country by their habit of dressing it heavily with a pomade in the shape with which the old Egyptian monuments have made us familiar. Here the rhinoceros certainly fulfils the mission of the ox, as I can testify from actual observation in this home of the lion, the panther, the giraffe, the bear, and the

BEFORE HE CAN TURN, THE HUNTER BURIES A SPEAR IN HIS HEART.

zebra, and so many other animals, besides reptiles and birds, interesting to a naturalist. I had hired a dahabieh at Cairo, and, with my faithful Thursday as

THE RHINOCEROS FULFILS THE MISSION OF THE OX.

servant, joined another boat bound up the Nile. I planned to go at once as far as Assouan, where the first cataract of the Nile is, and where the country of the Barabras begins; and that from that point I would be governed by circumstances. It is seventy-five leagues or so from Cairo to Assouan, and travelling as we did, only by day. it took us a month. — one of the pleasantest of my life. The shores are lined with ruins. broken monuments, temples. and palaces of the Pharaohs, that fill the most unimaginative with delightful dreams of the past.

One day I was taking a nap in the comfortable cabin of my craft, when I heard loud cries of native children on the bank, and at the same moment Thursday came running in to call me on deck.

"What's all this row about?" grumbled I.

"Come and see the wicked beast with a tusk on the end of his nose!"

I left the boat by the plank that connected us with shore. to find a rhinoceros led by a party of Abyssinians, who made him perform antics like a trained dog. He would stand on his hind legs, lie down, get up, and dance at command, grunting with apparent admiration of his own accomplishments. His keepers assured me, through an interpreter, that it was not an uncommon sight in their own country. and that they had put the rhinoceros to all sorts of more useful employments.

It was on this trip that I had a narrow escape from falling into the jaws of "the river horse." — hippopotamus, one of the largest of mammals. This animal can never have been very common on the lower part of the

ON THE BACK OF THE FEMALE RESTED A YOUNG ONE, UGLIER, IF POSSIBLE, THAN ITS FOND PARENTS.

river, for you do not see his easily recognized figure among the hieroglyphics with which the temples are filled, between the Delta and the first cataract. Nor does Roman history often mention them in the games or triumphs of the emperors, which is singular, when tigers, lions, and elephants figure so often. But farther up the river you meet him still, usually swimming very low in the water, with simply his nose, eyes, and ears above its surface, and followed by his mate. — for they travel usually in couples. But on the day to which I refer. this number was increased to three. — and huge specimens they were, — sunning themselves on the left bank of the river, and on the back of the female rested a young one, uglier, if possible, than its fond parents. We were six of us, only one a native. rowing along the shore in a skiff; and one of my companions. a Frenchman, with the careless thoughtlessness of his race. raised his rifle and let drive at the youngster. There was a tremendous splashing and racket, and the water for yards was stirred up by the four mighty bodies diving into it simultaneously. A cry of warning came from our guide. who began jabbering away in his own lingo at a great rate.

"What's the beggar raising all this row about?" asked the Frenchman.

"Pull for your life!" shouted I. "You'll have the whole party round us in a minute."

The boat was a poor one for speed, and we were still a long way from the nearest point of land when the snouts of the hippopotami came to the surface within pistol-shot of the stern. In a moment they were around us, threatening to crush the thwarts of our craft and make two mouthfuls of the whole party. We dropped our oars — for flight was out of the question — and seized our guns. Placing my barrel almost against the eye of the largest, I emptied both barrels into his head, and he sank without a gurgle into the muddy water. Meanwhile the other end of the boat had been less fortunate. The remaining male had fastened his massive jaws in the gunwale and was crunching it like paper, while the Frenchman. the cause of all the danger, was ineffectually belaboring his head with an oar, his empty gun being, of course. useless.

Luckily for us. one of the party had a loaded rifle and some presence of mind left, and to these hippopotamus number two reluctantly yielded. and went to join his friend at the bottom of the muddy river. It is really curious how easily and quickly so huge an animal will die under modern weapons. when you remember what difficulty the ancients experienced in killing large game, and how an entire army was needed to cope with an elephant or hippopotamus. But to return to our still rather unpleasant predicament: before the female could reach us. we were all reloaded and ready for her. She seemed to realize this, for. without waiting for our cordial reception. she turned tail and made for the other shore, leaving a wake behind her like a harbor steamboat. Reaching

THE FRENCHMAN WAS BELABORING HIS HEAD WITH AN OAR.

a long tongue of land near the farther bank, she waded through the shallows and across it, disturbing the croco-

DRIVING THE CROCODILES INTO THE WATER.

diles sunning thereon, and driving them into the water beyond, into which she followed them and was lost to our sight. And not one of the party seemed to care!

# CHAPTER XI.

 NCE Hanno. Emperor of Carthage, on returning from a campaign covered with the trophies of victory. glittering in gold and silver, stood before his captives. There were five hundred of them, naked. chained together. bowed under the yokes which ground into their shoulders, standing silent before their master. Between him and them was a blazing brazier. Other slaves. older in years of servitude, were heating the irons with which the mark of slavery was to be branded in the quivering flesh of the captives.

"Stop!" said he. with an imperious gesture. "Let half of the *beasts* stand on my right. and half on my left. Now. let those on my left get together the material and build me a palace more magnificent than any in Carthage; and those on my right. away with them to the desert. and let them bring me home young lions — scores of them, and quickly."

They were free! — two hundred and fifty men. Under guards they departed for the southern part of the province, where they laid skilfully arranged traps for the "King of the Desert." They lay in ambush, armed

with spear and arrow; and when the old lions fell into
the pitfalls, they rushed upon the young, and by heroic
struggles, body to body and limb to limb, captured the

HE AND HIS SUITE APPLAUD THEIR BLOOD-THIRSTY FEROCITY.

means to freedom.  What feverishly anxious nights they
must have passed! what long, hot days!  If one of the
lions only was taken, and the other returned while

they were fighting the young. the odds became terrible against the would-be captors. A hundred were killed and many more wounded ; but eighty young lions were brought back to please the powerful emperor. who put them in a magnificent cage he had had built especially for his pets. Then, turning to the unfortunate slaves. he said disdainfully. —

"Here is excellent food for my lions!"

Not a day passed but he and his suite were present at his favorites' feast on human flesh. to watch their cat-like gracefulness. and applaud their blood-thirsty ferocity. As they grew larger the emperor had their teeth filed down and their claws cut. and the trainers put into the cage to teach them docility and prepare them for his own royal coming. In a few weeks he was able to spend hours in the pleasure of their company, his own tastes and passions proving a bond of sympathy with these fierce mates. More than this, in a glistening chariot drawn by twenty of the handsomest lions, he drove through the rich quarters of Carthage carrying terror before him, and handling his curious team with a firm rein. while he smiled to see his subjects fly in fear at his approach. From these wild drives he returned to his palace satisfied with such glory.

Meanwhile the Senate and people met, and, after brief deliberation, decreed that Hanno should be exiled, under the pretext that he who could subjugate the lion might think of doing the same to the freeborn citizen.

Some years later, Mark Antony renewed the fancy of the African monarch. He showed himself to the Roman people in a chariot drawn by Numidian lions. Everything about this man was African, — his manners, his table, his mistress, his death even. Once acclimated in the Rome of the Cæsars, the king of the desert was in congenial surroundings, well lodged and well fed. It was in the arena of the Circus Maximus, less hot but more deadly than the African sands, that his strength was in future to be employed. Pompey was just made consul for the second time, and, in celebration of the event, he held a *Venatio* in that monster circus, where four hundred thousand spectators could be comfortably accommodated. Pompey himself presides in his private box, and at a signal from him, the gladiators, in national costume, wearing simply a glaive, and carrying a long spear, are introduced, to the sound of music. With them come a crowd of augurs, extemporizing on the good or evil fortunes in store for the warriors. Meanwhile the long procession is moving around the podium in honor of the twelve protecting deities. This first ceremony having been duly accomplished, and the customary salutes given the consul, as master of the games, the cages are opened. Then, to the applause and shouts of the people, fiercer, as Varro says, than the animals themselves, six hundred lions rush from the ten dens. They come with a confident air, sure of themselves and their reception, and divide, on opposite sides

of the arena. into two camps, nearly equal in number.
A shout like the roar of the sea, half smothered, is
uttered here and there by the more impatient gladia-

HIPPOPOTAMI.

tors, but most of them stand watching and taking the
measure of the opponent they have selected.  The spectators hang upon their every movement, with beating

hearts and panting breath. The actors are holding their audience spellbound in suspense!

Gradually the combatants approach, and, with a bound, engage in a terrible struggle. At the first shock the weakest bite the dust. Drunk with blood, the rest vent their rage upon the nearest foe or friend. To see them tear and bite, one would imagine they were revenging the murder of a friend or dearly loved mate. They seize one another by the throat; every muscle strains as they rend each other in pieces. It is frightful! It is one continued roar, lit up, like a thunder-cloud, by the piercing cries of the wounded and the mad shouts of encouragement from the people. The dead bodies strew the arena, crimsoned with blood and whitened with froth, while dying glances are cast toward the pitiless benches, where every Roman has selected his favorite to praise if he dies well, to curse him if he does not.

The applause dies away, and a rapt and concentrated attention shows itself on every cruel face. But twenty lions remain! Suddenly from all quarters comes the cry, —

"The elephants! Bring in the elephants!"

Once more the sound of grating doors is heard, and the new champions enter the lists, swinging their trunks, and with angry eyes scanning the lower benches. Which will conquer in this final strife? The elephants crush by their simple weight; the lions depend on their quicker movements and sharp fangs. You hear the cracking of broken bones, the spurting of blood, the sickening death-rattle. The ground is piled with dead and dying. The elephants can hardly stand, and the lions have retreated into one corner.

Suddenly the leader of the elephants reopens the fight. With a rush as irresistible as the tides, he charges upon the largest lion, and seizing him around the middle with his mighty trunk. he lifts him high as the tribunes' seats, and hurls him down a lifeless mass among his friends again. Instantly they leap at hazard upon the heads of their foes, and fasten their teeth and claws in any soft spot they can find. only to be crushed against the side of the arena by the agonized elephants. And now, into this nearly equal struggle, comes a third enemy — man ! A band of gladiators attack elephant and tiger alike with their redoubtable swords, avoiding the maddened beasts, and dealing deadly blows to right and left. The victory evidently will be theirs, when suddenly the elephants, wild with pain, turn, like bulls, upon the barriers which protect the cruel spectators ! They wish to try their strength with the cowards who have caused this needless slaughter. A panic ensues. Even Pompey grows pale as he sees the terrible vengeance with which his brutal subjects are threatened by his less brutal brutes. Human blood is evidently to run in the sands already dyed deep in gore, when, at a fortunate moment, a handful of slaves reinforces the gladiators, and the danger is past. A great sigh of relief goes up from the circus. and the *enjoyment* of the day is complete!

A FAMILY OF TAPIRS.

These disgraceful spectacles lasted in Rome for four hundred years, and resulted in the butchery of over cne hundred thousand lions, besides tigers and elephants to an equal number. Persia. Asia Minor. and Arabia were delivered from these dangerous wild animals. and it is now very difficult to study the habits. especially of the first, except in menageries and, wild. in the south of India, Algeria, and Arabia. It was in the latter country that I had an adventure that proved conclusively to my mind the curious lack of maternal instinct in the lion, in which respect, as in so many others, this overestimated animal compares unfavorably with the elephant, — the real king of beasts.

One fine September morning. before sunrise, I left the charming village of Saïda. a favorite resort of Arabians. accompanied by two Arab horsemen devoted to my service. We were mounted on superb horses, — types of those for which the country is famous, — and travelled at a break-neck pace. The river, which flows from the high plateaus toward which we were riding. makes a sudden turn through the range of mountains just above the village to which it gives its name. and flows deep below in a gorge covered in with vines and laurel blooms. After riding a regular steeple-chase for fully an hour, we were obliged to proceed at a slower pace, as the soil became more sandy and the sun hotter. At last we were brought to a stand-still by the heat, and decided to rest in the shade of one of the groups of trees that here and there dotted the desert. One of my companions was telling an interminable story worthy of the Arabian Nights, when suddenly our horses ceased their pasture, tossing their heads with distended nostrils, and showing by the trembling of their muscles that some large enemy that they feared was not far away.

In an instant we were in the saddle, ready for anything, with our guns lying across the necks of our horses. We rode them behind a group of rocks a little farther on, and lay in ambush to see what was approaching. I stood up in my stirrups, but could not discern a movement anywhere in the bushes; but after an hour of tedious waiting in the hot sun, a tremendous roar, followed by sharp whines and angry growls, came from the little oasis we had just left. Fifty paces from us appeared two lions, a male and a female. It was more than we had hoped for, and, in spite of a hunter's courage, I confess I felt a not unwarranted nervousness. To be sure, we were three to their two, but even that consolation was almost immediately taken away from us! The female lay on a couch of leaves, and near her stood her lover, caressing her in true feline style, when, with a roar like the ocean, a tremendous male sprang from the thicket and stood with quivering tail and angry eyes before his rival. He was the stronger of the two, but the first did not hesitate; and at a kind of signal cry from the fair one, they fell upon one another in fearful fashion. Each tried to throw the other off his feet upon the ground to bite him. Their

claws buried in each other's sides drew blood at every
blow.  By a feint full of grace and agility the smaller
lion evaded the embrace of his enemy and sunk his fangs

NEAR HER STOOD HER LOVER, CARESSING HER.

deep in his flanks.  Over and over they rolled. and each
movement brought them nearer us.  We had all we could
do to hold our horses, and at last, at a given signal, three

rifles cracked, followed by terrible roars, and the two lions fell side by side, dead. The female sprang to her feet to the rescue of her lovers, but her second bound was her last, and she too joined " the greater number " and lay beside her Romeo. My two Arabs proceeded to skin the prizes, — all very fine specimens, and one of them of singularly large size, — and to dress the favorite parts for supper. I must confess, to my shame, that I never admired the flavor or texture of lion steaks, and I turned into the thicket to find something more to my taste. Along the river I shot a brace of ducks and a superb grebe which I was carrying back toward camp. when, in a large fissure in a calcareous rock. I saw three young lions on a bed of leaves. They were lying across one another, like kittens, and were evidently quite well grown. I climbed down into the crevice. and, what was my astonishment, found them all dead, — strangled. either by the mother, to whom, in her new loves. they had proved an annoyance, or by the father, in a sudden burst of anger. We carried them out of their nest. and their skins added to the already large load with which we set out again for Saïda the next morning.

The tiger, to whose rarity I have above referred, is to my thinking a more royal beast than the lion, for what he loses in size and brute strength. he more than makes up in grace, agility, and address. That this is generally accepted in countries where he lives is proved by the adjective " royal " which is always coupled with

WE TRAVELLED AT A BREAKNECK PACE.

his name; but it is an adjective uttered with terror, and not respect; it is the royalty of the tyrant, and not the king. To him women and children even are not sacred, and he sacrifices them with truly Homeric carnage. Like a wolf in the sheepfold he enters the houses of some of the native villages, killing for the mere pleasure of seeing and tasting warm blood, like that king of old who killed two hundred chickens that he might have a perfect soup! Caring only for the freshest-killed meat he disdains anything else, and when hunger torments him again he rushes to new hecatombs. Like all the cat family, he never thinks of the morrow, but, in real Bohemian fashion, lives for to-day only.

In one of these little Indian villages, where even yet fire-arms are a cause of wonder and envy, a large man-eating tiger — Doo-lu-Shad-uce, in their lingo — had for several nights in succession visited the different houses, and hardly a family but mourned the loss of some member of its circle. The tiger carried his audacity so far as to come in broad daylight, and, like a wolf in the fold, entered the houses while the men were in the fields, and killed right and left.

I was in the neighborhood, and hearing of it, took Thursday and my two best rifles, and went to the natives' aid. These poor devils had relied on their sorcerer's incantations to avert the evil spirit; and he was now at his wits' end, and glad to see us, you may be

sure. I have always respected a man's religious opin-
ions; and I resolved. if possible. while ridding the country of a monster. to do it in such a way as to reflect
the greatest credit on the native beliefs, especially as
I saw that the priest's lack of success was appreciated
by the natives. and that they were evidently losing confidence in superhuman aid. preferring to trust to our
rifle-barrels as a stronger staff in the difficulty than the
religion in which every one should trust.

How to arrange it was the great question. The animal had tasted human blood. and was sure to return.
The very night before, while the incantations were going
on that were to free the village from his evil spirit, the
tiger had suddenly appeared in their very midst, fasten-
ing upon two of the chiefs at his first bound. and. in
spite of their struggles and their friends' spears, he had
carried one of them off, leaving the other disembowelled
on the ground.

At last an idea flashed upon me. I bought a fine,
healthy bull of one of the Indians. and at night, accompanied by my guide and the sorcerer, led him out to the
edge of the clearing, beyond the last hut of the village,
and tied him to a stout bamboo. on the side of the
road a dozen paces or less from one of the priest's
pools of hallowed water. with which at regular intervals he had surrounded the village. Into this basin
I poured a few drops from a flask I carried. — it is
needless to say *not* of brandy, — and then drew my

HE ENTERED THE HOUSES, AND KILLED RIGHT AND LEFT.

companions into a natural hiding-place behind a lot of water plants not unlike sugar-cane. I gave Thursday two rounds of ammunition, but cautioned him under no circumstances to fire without explicit orders from me when and how to do so. We had lain nearly an hour in this pleasant spot, drinking in malaria and marsh fever, when the tiger appeared. It was a beautiful moonlight night, and we could see him advancing at a stately pace, his wide black bands moving rapidly enough to give him the appearance of being entirely brown, just as the quick turning of a colored disk leaves only a white impression to the eye. He came with head up, a superb sight (see frontispiece), and when ten yards from us scented us, as well as the bull, and paused, evidently torn with conflicting desires, and uncertain how best to gratify his insatiable stomach, gorged with human blood from over forty victims the night before. His lips parted, showing a set of sharp, ugly teeth; his skin wrinkled, especially over his forehead; his nostrils quivered, distending to their widest at the prospect of such delicacies; and his eyes gleamed with cruel anticipation. It seemed, lying there within one of his bounds, as though he took a long time to decide. At length he crouched ready to spring, but whether upon the bull or us it was impossible yet to tell. My gun was at my shoulder, the barrel pointed between those wicked eyes. There was a moment of intense suspense. The poor bull tried to break away

from its chain, and failing miserably, uttered a heart-
rending sound, and lowered his horns toward the tiger
to ward off death for a little. at least. The tiger drew
himself together like a steel spring, and bounded upon
him with such force that he threw him upon his side;
then, climbing upon his massive shoulders. the cruel
beast opened his throat with the precision of a butcher.
and then lay flat on his stomach. in the midst of his
feast. The bull made ineffectual efforts to roll over
and smother his assassin. but the latter was not to be
shaken off. The blood poured into his thirsty throat
in great gulps; it was frightful to see. The tiger
revelled in delight. and seemed to long to be able to
swallow more quickly. One cannot conceive such vo-
racity. He had opened the stomach of the now pas-
sive bull, and absolutely swam in blood. tearing off
bits of smoking flesh here and there, in a terrible
frenzy, drunk with pleasure. and feverish with a name-
less lust.

Once cold, the body lay neglected; and the monster
turned to us! Could he be hungry after such a feast
of Sardanapalus? Probably not. In fact, we saw him
advancing slowly, his tongue hanging out, his eyes
heavy, his gait almost staggering, toward the pool of
holy water. which, when he reached, he buried his hot
head and flanks in its refreshing water, wallowing like
a "river horse" in its coolness. I could not help laughing aloud at the success of my plan, and my companions

IN SPITE OF THEIR STRUGGLES, HE CARRIED ONE OF THEM OFF.

looked at me in terror, thinking I had lost my senses under the last half-hour's excitement.

As the poison I had poured into the pool began to affect the beast, he uttered several piercing yet half-strangled cries, and, with a few rapid contortions, fell over dead.

The next morning the whole village assembled to do us honor, and express their admiration of our prowess; but, finding our guns had not been discharged, and that it was at the sacred pool that the "man-eater" fell, they experienced that religious terror to which uneducated races are so susceptible, and bowed before the priest, whom they found mightier than the beasts of the forest. This feeling was encouraged by my giving him the skin and teeth of the tiger. — the former measuring four yards from nose to tail. — and we left them performing one of their curious dances in honor of their all-puissant deities.

They tell a queer story in India of an Englishman who came out to add a tiger's head of a certain size to his already large collection. He sought a district renowned for its immense tigers. armed simply with a long sharp dagger like those formerly carried in Venice. and a curious-shaped travelling box. When the latter was opened, it proved to contain a full suit of plate armor!

Clothed in steel from head to foot, dagger in hand. this — to say the least — original hunter walked at night.

like Hamlet's father on the platform, along the shore of a pond where game came to drink. On the second night a huge tiger sprang upon him from behind, and

THE TIGER STRAINED ITS JAWS ON THIS MAN OF IRON.

felled him at a blow. The cool Englishman lay perfectly still, feigning to be dead, while the tiger broke its claws and strained its jaws on this man of iron!

Finally, seeing just the right opportunity, the Englishman plunged his poisoned dagger deep into the tiger's heart, and the latter fell without a sound. When remonstrated with for waiting so long in such a dangerous embrace, he calmly replied: " I wanted to be sure that his head was exactly the right size before killing such a superb specimen, and having satisfied myself on this point, I waited a moment to strike home without injuring the part I was after!"

# CHAPTER XII.

## A LETTER FROM THE NIGER.

OTHING was too good for us in the eyes of the priest, who felt that he owed us much for the defence of his religious authority. and he set his parishioners the example by placing everything he owned at our disposal. Rice. tobacco, tea, and spices were offered us *ad libitum*. and every house seemed to wish the honor of lodging us.

Declining what we could without hurting their feelings. we lived partly on these delicacies, and partly on our own good stores. and continued on our way farther inland : for my hunting passion — like the tiger's thirst for blood — had been whetted by the night's adventure, and I longed for another sight of this terrible wild beast. Before night I reached the home of a powerful rajah whom I had before visited, and whose hospitality I had been able. in slight way. to repay. He welcomed me with the pomp of an Oriental reception. An army of servants was immediately placed at my orders, and a state hunt appointed for the next day. These gala ceremonies are always offered to strangers whom the Indians wish to honor, however short their visit may be.

At break of day we set out in an imposing array.
Twelve elephants, brilliantly trapped, bore the rajah,
the principal officers of his suite, and your humble ser-

A GUEPARD, OR HUNTING TIGER.

vant, lying, like the Romans at their feasts, on our
backs, under the howdahs. Beside us lay several good
rifles, and behind each of us, his eyes bandaged, a

guepard, or hunting tiger. This curious animal, half-tiger, half-leopard, is famous for his extraordinary eye-sight, his speed in running, and his courage in attack. At the same time he is a thoroughly good-natured and submissive companion, and makes a capital hunter besides.

There were some hundred men in the party, besides porters, servants, and cooks, and we journeyed by short stages in really royal style. No one ever complains of the sleepy slowness of an elephant's gait. You enjoy the scenery, you are rocked by his gentle movement into the happiest frame of mind, and you "get there."

After three days of this ideal travelling, one of our advance couriers came in to say that a tiger was reported in the neighborhood of one of the near villages, and we all prepared for an exciting day. I had my rifles cleaned and my ammunition and knives inspected, and resolved to give a good account of myself. We found that the tiger carried off daily a bull from the fields, and escaped with it into a densely grown marsh a few miles away. Hardly had we reached the locality before the guepards gave unequivocal signs that they detected the presence of our game. Armed with spears, the men began to beat the bushes, much as if they were simply after hares. Still, as they did not seem to mind the danger, I could not see why I should worry about them, though I sat ready with gun in rest on my elephant's back.

The plan was successful; for two enormous tigers, as large as the one I had "enchanted," bounded out of the high underbrush like young cats. Our men's cries and the general hubbub confused them and made them lose their heads, and they ran back and forth without any plan or method. Suddenly one of them sprang at my elephant, full in the face. as is their favorite method of attack. Before I could come to the rescue with my rifle, the noble beast had calmly torn the brute from its hold, hurled it upon the ground, and placed his ponderous fore-feet, one on its flanks and one

THEIR FAVORITE METHOD OF ATTACK.

on its head! I felt a violent jerk and shock, and heard the cracking of bones like the sound of a tree broken by the force of the tempest; and I saw the beast flattened under the weight of the massive pachyderm. The latter, proud of his deed, never lost his dignity or temper for an instant, and I showered caresses and sugar upon him in reward for his prompt courage. Meanwhile the other tiger had not remained inactive. He had succeeded in bringing down a young elephant, on which was mounted a son of the rajah, now on his first hunt; the latter, however, had the good sense to desert his mount, and leave the poor thing to its fate.

Immediately we all let loose our guepards, which fell upon the prey with their sharp teeth and indomitable courage. The fight became general: the wounded tiger held its own against the numerous foe, putting several *hors du combat*, laying them open with its fearful claws, or meeting its fangs in their throats. The struggle was intense, and the rajah's enjoyment of it was too, for he would not let me end it with a shot from my good rifle. After some minutes of this kind of thing he gave his men a signal, and they surrounded the combatants and with their spears put an end to the tiger, and drew off the limping guepards.

On my return I found the following letter from an old hunting companion in Africa : —

My DEAR FRIEND. — There are days when I envy you your lot. In the immense plains of the Ganges you meet only enemies that attack openly, and from whom you fear no surprise ; but here everything is different. As you know, we have to fight and watch constantly ; and it is not the natives that annoy us the most, for a few shots will drive them away. In fact, on the banks of the Niger all is not roses. In the first place, there is the terrible fever which you draw in at every breath, and to which the strongest man succumbs in two days. You have had a touch of it yourself, and will remember. There is besides another foe — the leopard — with which the country is infested; and knowing your fondness for hunting adventures, I will write you of this traitorous enemy, whom you have met so often.

I started on an expedition last October, as I wrote you, taking a thousand men,. infantry and marines, from several regiments stationed at St. Louis. Some native tribes encamped between the Senegal and the Niger were to be vigorously punished for having intercepted supplies and insulted explorers of the upper Niger.

This delicate mission was confided to me, and I was not sorry to get into active warfare again. We marched by easy stages, carrying a month's provisions. One hundred of my men had charge of a herd of cattle and sheep which we took with us, and from which, each day, we obtained our fresh meat. The very first day out, the adjutant commanding this important four-footed division came to me, pulling his mustache in consternation, to say that ten head of sheep had disappeared, and that he could not, for the life of him, tell where or how. The guard had been posted and relieved as usual, and the men were as much annoyed as their officer. I was puzzled over this and subsequent daily thefts from our live-stock, both cattle and sheep, by the dozen, and began to fear that the crafty natives were following us and taking advantage of the darkness and their knowledge of the forest to steal our supplies; and I resolved to surround our stock-yard with an added number of guards. They had orders to close in as soon as they saw the mysterious thief and surround him. About midnight I was aroused by the lieutenant calling into my tent, "It is a leopard; shall we fire?" Hardly taking time to dress, I seized my rifle and hurried out after him, to convince my rather sceptical mind of his information. It was light enough to read, and a superb moonlight night. We found the sentinels at their posts, the cattle sleeping, and everything quiet! I laughed at the lieutenant and his false alarm, which made leopards out of shadows.

"No," said he, "I saw the leopards as clearly as I see you. They run at the least noise, never wishing to risk their spotted hides if they can help it; and I *know* I was not mistaken."

I felt sure the young man was at fault, but turned back to my tent, simply cautioning him to keep on the alert and report any further alarm at once. Just as I reached my canvas home, an enormous body fell, without the least warning, from the thick foliage above it, landing a few feet away from me. It was a leopard; and had it fallen upon me, I should not now be describing the fact to you, for he would have crushed me as flat as a pancake. I called for help, and at the same time discharged my rifle, aiming for his glowing eyes. The shot told, and he rolled over dead. Several shots followed immediately from the sentinels, and the whole camp ran out to see what was up. In a moment we were on the field of action. A

SEVERAL SPRANG UPON OUR SOLDIERS.

dozen leopards, that had lain in ambush behind tree trunks and branches like sharpshooters, had instinctively betrayed themselves at the noise of shooting, and had taken flight at hazard among the guards. When we arrived the excitement was at its height. The leopards, wounded, and held in a circle of gun-barrels that they could not break, were using all their agility to get through our lines. Several sprang upon our soldiers and tried to strangle them. One corporal was completely laid open, and we had the greatest difficulty in saving him from his furious foe in this mangled condition. Two other men saved themselves at close quarters by using their revolvers, and one his sabre; and my tent is now softly carpeted with seven magnificent leopard skins, the results of the fray.

My friend's letter reached me at an unfortunate time for reply; and I had arrived at Java — that country so rich in archæological remains and animal life — before I could give it the attention it deserved. After matters of merely personal interest, I described to him, in return for his stories, an example of the curious veneration for some animals felt by the superstitious islanders.

"The Prince of Djokjokarta, a kind of Javan sultan, loved to surround himself with extravagant pomp. One day he started from his palace to visit his subjects, accompanied by a superb escort all robed in white. He was carried upon a magnificent dais, covered with gold and

precious stones. Four slaves waved perfumed fans of
ostrich feathers above his head, while others watched
his slightest beck and nod ; and before and behind him

BEFORE AND BEHIND HIM MARCHED AN INNUMERABLE TRAIN.

marched warriors, guides, and hunters, — an innumerable
train. The first night, as they were travelling through
the forest, they heard a dreadful noise above their heads
in the foliage of a large tree. It sounded like a panther :

and they immediately formed a hollow square around their sovereign to protect him from the dangerous beast, while a noted hunter, named The Sun, advanced a few steps to see what threatened them. His long lance with its silken and golden handle was beside him, and he was ready, if necessary, to die for his king. Suddenly disorder ran through the ranks; the torches were unexpectedly extinguished; every one cried out and gesticulated, and fell upon the supposed enemy, and wounded one another, until a terrible shriek pierced the night, followed by intense silence. Then The Sun relit his torch, and was horrified to find, in a pool of blood, a sacred monkey, dead and stiff; and a laugh went up from all the frightened men, but the Prince sat silent and grave.

"'Who has killed this inoffensive animal?' thundered he.

"'It is I, great Prince; I pierced him with my lance, to protect you from danger.'

"'Who authorized you to shed blood?'

"The Sun hung his head in silence; and at a sign from the despot, he was seized by the soldiers, and chained to a cart that followed the procession. He knew that death was the invariable penalty for wounding one of these venerated animals, and although he was a great favorite of the sultan, he could hope for no mercy.

"When the journey was ended he was called before his master, who said, —

"'If I give you your liberty, what will you do with it?'

" And the abject Sun replied, —

" ' Light of the Day, I will devote it to adoring you.'

" Now the next day was one of fête, and, to add to its festivities, the judges of the people decided that The Sun should undergo the proof from the black panther, and if he got out of the unequal contest alive, he should be reinstated in his honors as guiltless.

" The Prince approved this judgment. feeling confident in his favorite minister's courage and strength, and left the choice of arms to him.   He selected the short Ceylon poniard and a bit of wood shaped like a dumb-bell.

" Toward the end of the day, when its heat was somewhat spent, the amusements began in the court-yard of the palace.   A light tent was drawn over it, and from the cornices hung marvellous stuffs from Eastern looms. The Prince made his entry on a tremendous elephant, lost beneath a pile of sumptuous trappings. and surrounded by all the court dignitaries. with their servants and bearers.   When the Prince dismounted they threw themselves down upon the ground. and he walked upon their prostrate forms to his seat, whence he viewed the marvellous dancing of his nautch girls.

" After the sensuous. the cruel.   Two men, their heads covered with turbans, and wearing masks with eyeholes, appeared, each with a long rod.   They drew near, and after crossing rods like fencers, began to lash one another in rhythmical time, as if they were hammering iron.   Under each swishing blow the flesh writhed and the blood

SHE FASTENED HER CRUEL TEETH AND CLAWS DEEP IN HIS NECK.

spurted. It was a horrible sight, brought to an end when one of the contestants acknowledged he could stand no more. It was impossible to tell by appearance which the victor was, so sore and scarred were they both.

"Finally a cage was dragged out, in which was a magnificent black panther, as large as a tiger. He seemed timid before so many people and such bright lights, and had to be urged out from behind his bars with a goad, and even then took refuge behind a post, where the buffalo, let loose to fight him, attacked him furiously. It was evident at once which would be the victor. The buffalo went like a shot from a rifle, burying his horns in the flanks of the panther, and crushing him against the palisades, goring him through and through. He uttered but one cry, and was dead.

"The Prince ordered another panther freed. It was a female, smaller and fiercer than the first, that came running in, like a cat in haste. Her eyes glowed viciously, and instead of waiting an attack, she sprang at a bound above his head, and fastened her cruel teeth and claws deep in the back of his neck. The bull made a thousand turns to free himself of this foe that was sapping his very life. He rubbed against the palisade, he rolled over and over upon the ground, he sprang clumsily into the air; but the panther stuck as if riveted to him. At last the great animal succumbed, sinking in his own blood, in which the ferocious panther positively revelled, wallowing in gore, and tearing her prey in pieces. Indeed, so reluctant was she to let go that she was dragged the length of the arena by the attendants as they removed the remains, and was safely locked up with them in her cage again.

"Now the time was come for the proof of The Sun. who entered with the simple arms he had chosen, and placed himself facing his king. whom he saluted. One could not help admiring his coolness, as he stood with folded arms awaiting the test; the panther was loosed from the opening at the opposite end of the arena, his hair on end, his back *creasing* like a cat's, ready for a leap. his tongue protruding between his gleaming teeth. Suddenly he drew himself together. and unbent like a spring, bounding in a graceful curve upon his prey. The shock must have been frightful, but it did not overthrow the man, nor did he lose his presence of mind. With his left hand he forced the wooden block between the angry jaws. which closed upon it. and with his right he buried his poniard in the beast's shoulder. The latter fell in a limp heap. tearing The Sun's knee with his claw as he fell. This was his only wound; and he had strength to reach his despot's throne. and be received back into favor by this easily convinced monarch. For my own part, I prefer to trust to the average jury!"

# CHAPTER XIII.

## ANOTHER OF THE CAT FAMILY.

 WAS fishing when Thursday, his hair standing on end and his eyes like the setting sun, came running toward me. He was breathless and speechless.

"Have you seen the ghost of your ancestor?"

He shook his head, but still could not speak. Evidently something serious was the matter. All he could do was to point to a little island left in the stream by the falling waters, but about which I could see nothing extraordinary. When I started to move in that direction, the one from which he had just come, he grasped me firmly. and nothing could shake him off. "Let me go, coward!" said I; "or at least let us climb into this tree. where we can see something besides these everlasting marshes." The idea seemed to strike him, for in a twinkling he was in the lower branches of the tree, where I rejoined him, and where a curious sight greeted me. A jaguar, the fiercest of the cat family, was a few yards away peacefully engaged in *fishing*. I could hardly believe my eyes. But there he crouched, — an enormous specimen fully six feet long besides his tail, that would measure a yard more, watching with his piercing eye the water below him.   He was absolutely motionless, and you would have thought him stuffed; but his jaws rested almost on the surface of

THE JAGUAR PEACEFULLY ENGAGED IN FISHING.

the stream, and upon its waters there fell noiselessly the saliva, to which the fish will rise as to a bait, whereupon he struck them on to the beach with a sure aim that never failed to land his game. In an hour I saw him catch fifty of different sizes. with the same instinct and pleasure that a house-cat catches the gold-fish.

Suddenly the scene changed. The avenger of the innocents appeared in the shape of a number of crocodiles. In an instant twenty open jaws rose from the surface of the water and moved toward the jaguar. who retreated slowly into the brake, followed by the crocodiles. Upon the leader. who was a monster, the jaguar pounced, tooth and nail, and tried to sink his fangs into the unyielding armor of his hide, while the crocodile wound his snake-like body around the foe, and strained every muscle to strangle him. Never did I see a finer wrestling bout; and the jaguar was getting the best of it, when the crocodile's friends came to the rescue. like dogs upon a quarry. Soon a dozen lay dead, all killed in the same way, — their throats cut clear across with a jagged tear. through which the blood poured and their breath escaped in uneven gasps like puffs from a bellows. The jaguar limped. and could hardly stand ; for the terrible amphibians had crushed his haunches, breaking the bones and dislocating the joints. He killed now simply for the pleasure of killing. The sight and smell of blood intoxicated him, and when the few remaining crocodiles. wounded and terror-struck, undertook to escape into the stream again, he assumed the offensive and barred their retreat. With a few blows from his claws he added them to the slain, and remained victor on the field of battle. But his triumph was short.

Even while he was slaking his fever in long draughts from the yellow stream, his bloody jaw dropped, his eyes lost their light, and he rolled over dead, in the very spot where I had watched him fishing at first.

I took pleasure in making the cowardly native take off his magnificent skin, which decorates my study floor as I write.

It was the beginning of the rainy season. Twenty servants accompanied me, carrying provisions, arms, and ammunition; and my hunting-fever being on me, I was resolved to see more of this interesting and beautiful animal, the jaguar.

The forest proved to be of an almost impenetrable luxuriance, and the problem seemed to me to reach any game, even when we knew they were near. I almost resolved to try our old plan in Ceylon, where the same conditions prevail, — of setting fire to the woods on three sides of a square and stationing the hunters on the fourth.

The native ingenuity overcame this difficulty when the time came, — namely, the second afternoon after we had gone into camp. The peculiar cry of a jaguar was heard at some distance in the forest, and immediately my head guide detailed a native to perform the feat of drawing him toward us. This fellow, naked save the cloth around his middle, climbed a tall tree near us, like a squirrel. From this height, seated astride a branch, he began to imitate the calls and sobs of a young monkey in distress.

ONE MORE SKILFUL THAN THE REST CAUGHT HIS NOOSE AROUND HIS HIND QUARTERS.

He did this perfectly, but so loud did it sound in the now silent forest — for the jaguar's cry had ceased instantly — that I could not help fearing he had scared away the prize.

"Do not believe it," said Thursday. "These fellows know what they are about, and you will see the brute drop upon our friend in a few minutes, like a stroke of lightning."

"But the poor fellow has no arms. He will be killed."

Thursday shrugged his shoulders nonchalantly, as if "who cares?"

Hardly had he finished when the native uttered a piercing shriek, and a terrible hand-to-hand struggle began in the tree-top. The jaguar had approached silently, by light bounds from branch to branch, and when within reach made one last one upon the supposed monkey. Great confusion reigned. The natives rushed frantically round the base of the tree, trying to lasso the beast, when they caught sight of his spotted hide through the leaves. Finally one more skilful than the rest caught his noose around the hind quarters of the jaguar, and brought him down limb by limb, but directly upon himself. We could not get a shot without killing the man; and his friends, whose lassos would have done good service, fled incontinently and left him to his fate. The jaguar, fortunately, was well held, and every frantic bound he made to free himself tightened the noose and slowly strangled him. Watching our opportunity, in one of these leaps, Thursday and I gave him each our quota of cold lead, and he fell dead beside the native.

I supposed the latter, too, was killed, of course; but not at all. His shoulder was laid open, but not badly, and after a few days he was round with the rest, against whom he seemed to harbor no ill-will for their cowardliness.

A great American hunter, whose books are famous, told me that the jaguar is harmless enough until he sees or tastes blood. Then nothing will control him; he is mad for more, and simply kills blindly to satisfy this passion. He told me, that returning one day from the fields he had found three negroes lying in their blood, and a pet jaguar, that had always seemed perfectly submissive and friendly, hidden behind some bags, ashamed of the fury that a sudden sight of flowing blood had occasioned in him. He looked for all the world like a dog that expected a thrashing for some fault.

"We have a wild-cat," said he, "beside which the jaguar is a lamb. I was travelling once among the Indians of South America, and came to a little village of a friendly tribe, where my party was most hospitably received. The best hut in the village and the best food and drink were given us with a grace civilization does not know. When we awoke in the morning the village was in an uproar, and all our friends bore signs of the liveliest distress on their faces. We found a great misfortune had fallen upon them. Part of their wealth had been annihilated. The meadow where they pastured their sheep had been visited by a wild-cat, a hundred

THREE NEGROES LYING IN THEIR BLOOD.

sheep left dead upon the plain, and the rest frightened away into the woods, where it was very difficult to find them.

" The Indians, true to their nature, swore revenge, and I remained a few days to see how they would accomplish it. The mighty hunters of the tribe arrayed themselves in sacks, in skins, and in coverings of leaves and moss, and lay in wait in the meadow among the dead sheep, and the squaws covered them over so completely they could hardly breathe, during the thirty hours they had to remain in hiding. All this time, of course, they were without food. But the second day, toward noon, the cat appeared; and we, in the huts, watched with eager eyes his stealthy advance from bush to bush. As soon as he reached the pasture he stopped, sniffing the air and glancing in every direction to see if he was observed. To make more sure he climbed a tree, and sat there watching several minutes. Seeing nothing he sprang at a bound to the earth to resume his gorge. Immediately the Indians were up, and twenty arrows laid the thief low. He fell without a cry, and the hunters began a mad dance around his body, while the shouts and songs of the children and squaws showed the joy felt in the success of the *ruse*. The village divided the meat, which is too rank and gamey for me, and, with a little rum from my stores, made a wild night of it."

Seeing my interest in his stories, the American offered to tell me some curious adventures with bears, and during the next few days he amused me with those you will find in the next chapter.

TWENTY ARROWS LAID THE THIEF LOW.

# CHAPTER XIV.


## AN AMERICAN'S ADVENTURES.

" I WAS hunting in the mountains, rather aimlessly it must be confessed, when I ran across an old she-bear. bearing in her jaws a lot of roots and vegetables, as if returning from market. I followed her, for the bear seldom. if ever. attacks. unless outrageously provoked, and I was curious to see the family to which she was evidently taking this food. In a crevice in the rocks. near the top of a ledge, lay five — instead of the traditional three — cubs, and looking down upon them I saw her divide the delicacies with maternal impartiality among her tumbling offspring. She treated them in the most affectionate and caressing manner, and they answered her in like fashion. presenting a most charming family picture. Several days later I returned. to find the young scamps playing round the base of the cliff and the old lady away. They were like young dogs in feature and gentleness. but their color was a tawny yellow, relieved with a white necklace. They were apparently about two months old. and I resolved to kidnap two for domestication. I selected two at hap-hazard. and seizing them by the nape of the neck. dropped them into

a bag I had brought for the purpose, and carried them
off to my camp.   Later in the day I returned to see how
the family fared without two of its members, and I was

THE BEAR IN CAPTIVITY.

horror-struck at the sight I saw.   I was about to enter
the crevice, to find, as I supposed, the sleeping cubs.
when I perceived a huge animal at the back of the cave

*eating* its poor young! — eating with a gusto and drinking the warm blood greedily. I drew back and pushed a large stone against the entrance, and lighting my bag, which was, of course, hemp, and burned readily, I tossed it into the bed of dried ferns and leaves behind my improvised prison-bar. The dry stuff caught instantly, and the smoke and flame poured out of the cracks, while the unnatural father made frantic efforts to escape from the fiery furnace to which I had, without recourse, condemned him, and in which I had the satisfaction to see his bad deeds punished.

"When the unhappy mother returned, she wandered inconsolably over the country for a week and then disappeared. Soon after, I was in a neighboring town visiting a clergyman whose parsonage overlooked the parish burying-ground. He told me — with real apprehension, too — that ghosts had recently disturbed his household's quiet, and that it was all he could do to keep his superstitious servant from leaving him alone upon his haunted hearth. I interrogated Gertrude, and found that upon a tomb erected to one who had died without the sacrament, 'like a dog,' on two successive nights she had seen a ghost, nodding and prostrating himself in real ghostly fashion. I don't believe much myself in that kind of nonsense; and I resolved to watch with servant and master the next night, when, sure enough, the performance was repeated; but to my sceptical eyes, even at the distance of our window from the grave-yard, by a very earthly animal walking upon four legs. I could never have convinced either of them of this had not the servant come running in the next day at dinner-time to say that a bear was in the garden eating sweets stolen from my host's beehives, and on my pursuing him, *broom* in hand, had he not retreated through the fence into the grave-yard. It immediately occurred to me that this was our unhappy ghost, and I resolved to see if the death of the former would not relieve us of the presence of the latter.

" The priest readily consented, and I proceeded to lay my plans, after which I retired behind a garden-house and awaited developments. As I had expected, the bear returned after a few hours to finish his interrupted feast, glancing around suspiciously and advancing with the greatest caution, watching the windows of the parsonage and starting like a guilty thief at every noise. When he reached the scattered sweets he began to make away with them most gluttonously, at every gulp showing an increased pleasure in his feast and an added gayety of demeanor. After the last bit had disappeared he began a series of clumsy gambols like a dance, ending in his falling on his back with his legs in the air and his eyes closed in contentment — or sleep. Slipping from my hiding-place, I crept cautiously up and buried a knife deep in his shoulder where I knew it would do the most good. He never stirred. The parson was greatly sur-prised at my success, until I confessed that a quart of

SEIZING TWO BY THE NAPE OF THE NECK, I DROPPED THEM INTO A BAG.

good alcohol was really responsible for the ease with which Bruin had dropped asleep, and that it was an added argument against the use of stimulants!

EATING STOLEN SWEETS FROM MY HOST'S BEEHIVES.

" ' And now, my dear fellow,' said I, ' we will sup from broiled bear's feet, if Gertrude is as skilful a cook as I take her to be.'

"Gertrude distinguished herself, and prepared them to perfection : but she would not eat of them herself, because there was something human about their appearance; and although I told many stories of the brute's cruelty and very inhuman ways, nothing would alter her resolution, and we finished them easily without her!

"There is nothing more interesting or curious than the bear's life, — alone, in hiding among the rocks and deep in the lonely forests; and between him and the orang-outang there is a strong resemblance in instincts and intelligence. One of the most cruel varieties of bear is the white one found in Norway and Siberia, where, among the superstitious, he is credited with almost divine characteristics, and even his lonely way of life is considered a sign of profound wisdom. They bring him their criminals for judgment : and if the latter are uneaten after striking him on the nose, they are pronounced guiltless! The Siberians have a queer way of hunting the bear. One day I had landed at a small town, and found the people in a wild state of excitement. A bear had come from the neighboring woods and carried off a woman to his fortress, and, by chance, had selected the prettiest girl in the village and a recent bride. I advised an immediate pursuit of the ravisher, and headed a small party which, with the aid of dogs, was soon on his track. We had provisions for several days, and the hunters were all armed with small-bore guns and long knives at their belts, and their courage aroused for any emergency, far

I AIMED OVER A CROTCH, AND FIRED.

beyond its usually very gentle pitch. They felt like the avenging Greeks, and that their honor as fathers and husbands was at stake. We beat all the bushes, hunted all the caves, and scaled all the ledges, without stirring a mouse. The dogs trotted along in front with their ears down, as if no game were within a hundred miles; and the relatives of the stolen girl had begun to calculate how nearly their relative could, by that time, have been eaten, when one of our scouts ran in to say he had seen the bear. Under his guidance we soon reached the spot, and the dogs were let loose upon him without further delay. He stood upon his hind legs, and dropped heavily upon the dogs when they came within his reach, crushing and strangling several. But one or two caught him by the throat and stomach, and were only shaken off after they had drawn blood in no stinted streams.

" The bear uttered angry growls and advanced slowly upon us. Meanwhile the natives had set up crotches in the ground on which to rest their light guns, in which I took little stock, and were preparing to open fire on him when I interfered. My own heavier arm was loaded with ball, and, after waiting till he had come within modest range, I aimed over a crotch and fired, killing him instantly. The dogs rushed upon him, and we had to beat them off with our guns in order to get the body, which was carried in state to the village, and a regular feast inaugurated. The husband of the lost girl insisted on an immediate autopsy ; but not a particle of his better half could be found in Bruin's stomach, and he had to console himself with the skin, which was voted him by popular consent.

"We had hardly reached the village when the missing girl, her hair flying and garments torn, rushed in as if followed by his Satanic Majesty himself. It seems the bear had treated her most gallantly, giving her food in his mountain fastness, and watching her with the greatest apparent admiration and without offering her the least violence. In the morning, when the bear started on a foraging expedition, she escaped over the barriers he had left at the entrance to his den; and while we had been interviewing him, she had made the best of her way back to the village, running all the way.

"I had another bear adventure," continued my friend, "which resulted in the capture, alive, of a very large specimen. He had taken refuge in a hole beneath the roots of a mighty tree, where it was impossible to get at him unless we should dig him out like a rat; so I arranged nooses around the opening and placed my men at some distance from the tree, each holding an end of rope. When Bruin put out his head to see if the coast were clear, we drew our nooses tight around his neck and held him helpless. We took him into the town and, finally, on board the vessel, where he became thoroughly at home and a prime favorite of all the men, especially the cook, in whose quarters he was usually to be found,

warming himself lazily before the fire, and superintending
solemnly the culinary proceedings.

"We landed in Norway to coal; and the bear, whom

HIS HEAD WAGGING ABOVE THEM WITH REAL ELOQUENCE.

the men had named Romeo, followed his friend on shore
and accompanied him on his various marketing errands,
to the terror of all the orderly natives. He even went

so far as to follow him into a church during divine service, where fifty good people were performing their daily devotions. Turning suddenly, the cook was horrified to find Romeo no longer visible! Where could he have gone? A moment before he had been close on his master's heels, and now he was not to be found. Within a few moments, however, he reappeared, but in a most unlooked-for spot, — his great paws on the edge of the pulpit, and his head wagging above them with real eloquence! There was an immediate stampede among the congregation; and every man, woman, and child made headlong for the doors, without standing on the order of their going. This incident created a great scandal; and we were compelled to go elsewhere to refit, where we did not allow Romeo to go ashore, fearing some new escapade. Arriving home, the cook begged to be taken into my service permanently, so great had his attachment grown to the bear, and I readily consented.

" Romeo and my children soon became fast friends; and though my neighbors laughingly spoke of our house as ' the bear pit,' we did not greatly mind, but were proud of our distinguished-looking nurse! He would go silently down the hall in the morning to the nursery, and awake his little charges, and, when they were dressed, ask nothing better than to play with them by the hour, or walk beside them when they took their exercise; and I always noticed that nothing was inclined to molest such a well-guarded party!

THIS WAS THE LAD'S REGULAR COUCH.

"One cold winter night, a poor little child very insufficiently clad, and barefoot, came to our door to ask for alms. He was a bright, fearless little fellow. and between Romeo and himself it was a case of love at first sight. We gave the lad something to eat. and as soon as his hunger was satisfied, Romeo took him bodily, and carried him off to his own quarters, where he took him between his warm haunches and pillowed him on the soft fur of his breast. For many days this was the lad's regular couch. and he was always sure of a welcome and a share of whatever was best in Romeo's larder.

" By the way. I remember very well the first time I hunted a bear, and it may amuse you to hear it."

I assured him that it would. and he continued :—

" It was in the Tyrol ; and I had been reading. as boys will. most exciting books of hunting adventures, until my imagination was filled with them, and I resolved to imitate my heroes forthwith. I had a light double-barrelled shotgun, and armed with it, I set out one bright morning early. in search of *bears*. After walking several hours without seeing anything in the way of game larger than a robin, I met an old man, bent and worn. going toward the village. On seeing my sportsman-like equipment he stopped to ask me in search of what game I had come. and on my frankly telling him. he laughed long and loud.

" ' What. are there no bears now in this neighborhood ?'

"'Oh yes, but far from here, and living among rocks and forests, that, alone, you could never penetrate: and even if you did, with such a pop-gun you could do little more than *tickle* a bear:' and off he went laughing to himself.

"I must confess I felt rather crestfallen at his evident disrespect for my plans and arms, but I resolved to show him how he had misjudged both, by bringing back a bear to put him out of countenance.

"With this laudable object in view, I continued my route for some miles, when suddenly, joy and delight! I saw a veritable bear in the middle of the road, on his hind legs, and with a heavy stick in his fore-paws. I could hardly believe my own good fortune, and my hands trembled with excitement as I raised my gun and aimed at his shoulder, as I had heard one should. Bang! bang! went both barrels; and when the smoke cleared away, I looked expecting to find him dead as a door-nail, instead of which he was merely scratching his back as though a mosquito had bitten him: while I heard loud shouts of 'Murder! don't fire, it is *my* bear!' from behind a neighboring rock, whence issued an irate wandering minstrel, whose sole stock in trade, beside his instrument, was the brute in question!

"I became the laughing-stock of the country, and after pacifying my injured friend by the payment of ample damages, I was glad to leave the Tyrol until the matter should blow over.

"In a voyage to arctic seas that I once made. we fell in often with the polar bear. and became familiar with the appearance and habits of this handsome variety.

MY HANDS TREMBLED WITH EXCITEMENT.

Our ship was caught in the ice off the mouth of the Lena, and it was impossible to get on even had we not been well supplied with fresh provisions. It was a real

Switzerland of icy peaks and crystal ravines, clothed. in place of forests, with stalactites and stalagmites. firm as marble and glittering like diamonds. By aid of our conveyances. half-sled and half-boat. we could travel among these wonders. hunting and fishing. and there was not a man on board but enjoyed the life. which we made as like that of the Esquimaux as possible. Out of three white bear-skins I had made myself a suit, perfectly impervious to wind and weather. giving me much the appearance of the animals from which they were taken. Only my eyes were visible. and even they were protected from the cold by a veil.

"More trying by far to a traveller than the cold is the darkness. Those long nights. during which all Nature seems dead. are so wearisome. and fill the mind with ennui. and the body with lassitude.

"One day the doctor came to pay me one of the long visits which rendered life endurable during these hours of darkness. His cabin was next to mine. — for we had built huts and dug out caves in the ice, instead of remaining on board in the discomfort caused by the angle at which the vessel lay. — and he suggested our tunnelling the partition of ice between, that we might have a covered gallery connecting our rooms. I agreed, and we set to work instantly. hoping to grow warm during the exercise. We were nearly done. and were beginning to congratulate ourselves on the rapidity of our work, when, in reply to a vigorous blow of the hatchet. we heard dis-

ON A FLOATING CAKE OF ICE A FEMALE AND TWO STALWART CUBS.

tinctly a growl very like that of a dog aroused from a nap.

"'It's a bear,' said the doctor, calmly. 'If you want to add to your store of skins, it is a good opportunity.'

"'Don't you suppose he will attack us?'

"'Not unless you fire a gun in his ear. He sleeps, and sleeps soundly, and we have but to kill him in his dreams in good Homeric style.'

"'That seems rather cowardly, but we do need skins and meat, so perhaps the means are justified.'

"The bear lay rolled in a ball, and covered with a blanket of snow, so that it was hard to distinguish his outline. As a sudden noise might awaken him, we had to be careful in approaching him, to do so silently; but we held him sure. Standing one on either side of his head, at a signal we buried our axes in his skull, and killed him instantly, thereby obtaining a most welcome addition to our daily bill of fare, as well as securing another wrap against the cold. He was seven feet long, which is a size to which no brown bear attains; and his size and weight were more those of a fatted ox than a wild animal. The color of his hair was slightly yellow, rather than white, and it was long, thick, and delightfully soft. The men were so rejoiced at the feast of meat that followed this lucky find, that they spent all their time looking for polar bears, but without any success.

"As the days began to grow longer, however, and the ice to break up a bit, we had better luck. One of the first of these days we saw, on a floating cake of ice, a large female and two stalwart cubs, for whom she was fishing, diving for the prey, and bringing it up almost every time to her hungry offspring. Suddenly she made a bolder plunge into the waves, and then began a wild struggle with some larger foe. We hurried forward to see what it could be, guided by the breaking of ice, the spouting of the water, and the tremendous noise which the contestants made. The bear bayed like a dog, and gnashed her teeth with rage, seeming unable to land her prey. All at once we caught sight of what it was, — a seal, — which just then threw itself bodily out of the water, and lifting its weight upon its tail and hind flippers, tried to bite the terrible fisherman. I ordered my men to loose a dog that had been trained to this special work, and off he tore like a shot. Menaced thus from behind, the bear turned upon this new enemy, and allowed the seal to slip quietly into the water and escape. The dog stood a few paces off, and tried by barking and constant movement to distract the bear's attention, and turn it to his advantage; but the old lady was too quick for him, and moved with surprising agility for so large a body. Not content with this policy of defence she slowly advanced toward the furious dog, now grown careless of his own safety, and, when almost upon him, gave a heavy spring, and crushed him like an egg-shell beneath her enormous weight. We were still too far off to help the poor creature, and as any advance was slow over the

hummocks and across the open channels, I almost de-
spaired of getting a shot at the bear; when, instead of

THE BEAR MADE A WILD LEAP UPON THE NEAREST CANOE.

escaping as she might easily have done, she came directly
toward us, having apparently quite forgotten the seal.

"The polar bear is fierce and vindictive, and does not,
I found, fly, like other bears, when hunted; and I loaded

my rifle quickly as the distance between us lessened. A wide, open channel, however, interposed between us, — too broad for my crazy make-shift of a boat or for a shot accurate enough to kill. But the natives with me had their tiny canoes, and, without so much as by-your-leave, launched them and paddled toward the hoped-for prize. They sat upon the bottom of their frail crafts, with their limbs stretched out under the deck, while a double-bladed paddle supplied the motive power. Beside each lay a long javelin barbed with iron. These hardy fellows paddled in good order toward the other side. When almost there, the bear made a wild leap upon the nearest canoe, overturning it and drowning its occupant like a rat. A second Esquimau, who came to his aid, met a similar fate, his skull being broken by a blow from her formidable paw.

"The circle of foes thus broken, the bear might again have escaped; but her maternal instincts called her to the aid of her little ones, and turning quickly to look for them, she found herself face to face with two more enemies, and without the chance to meet and defeat them separately. They took advantage of this, and plied their spears from opposite sides, tingeing the icy waters with her life's blood, and killing her in sight of her little ones. The four natives left then raised the huge carcass on their canoes and brought it with rejoicing to the shore, on which we stood spectators of the cruel hunt; for, to me at least, the sympathy was all with the game."

HIS CLAWS DEEP BURIED IN HIS VICTIM'S NECK.

One more of my friend's stories, and then to return to warmer climes.

He said: "That reminds me.   I was hunting buffaloes

MOUNTING THE SPECIMENS.

in the Rockies, — when they were more numerous, too, than they are now, — and was lying in wait near a stream, where I hoped they would come to drink.   All at once I became conscious of the presence of another hunter after the same game, — a black bear, lying along a huge limb that overhung the favorite pool. He lay there so still that I should never have noticed him, had not my own attention been concentrated on the same spot.

" Two magnificent buffaloes strayed away from the herd browsing far out on the plain, and came slowly down the wind toward us, — I say *us*, for the bear and I evidently had the same object in view in coming there. I resolved to see the thing out, and, if possible, bag two birds at the same shot. The buffaloes waded into the pool, and when directly under him, and not till then, the bear dropped heavily down upon the male like a hawk on its prey. The great ruminant was utterly helpless. and his companion tried in vain to assist him by vigorous blows from his stout horns, which fell quite as frequently upon friend as upon foe. In spite of them both the bear hung firm, his claws deep buried in his victim's neck, while the latter charged madly up the bank, where he fell crushed by the weight and strangled by the embrace of the bear.

" Now was my turn, I thought; and, while he was putting the finishing touches to his prospective meal, I sent an explosive bullet into his skull, and he fell upon the buffalo as dead as he."

I found the American a delightful companion; and his stories of Australia — where he had spent years — induced

A GLIMPSE INTO THE MUSEUM.

me to make a brief visit to that interesting country, where the life. both animal and vegetable. is so unlike anything I had ever seen.

It is needless to say Thursday accompanied me. and that we went well armed and fully prepared to add to my already extensive collection. which a skilled professional was mounting and arranging for me at home. In fact, I was able to keep a number of taxidermists continually employed, mounting the specimens I sent back. My barn had been transformed into a natural-history museum ; the hay intended for living quadrupeds distending the skins of dead ones, shot over many a field under tropic suns. It would have given a nervous person a sad turn to go into the building at night, when the moonlight came in floods through window and skylight, falling upon gorilla and orang-outang and every known variety of ape, arranged systematically. and flanked by tiger and lion. bear and giraffe. rhinoceros and hippopotamus, in most picturesque confusion.

I longed to return to these treasures, but. before doing so. turned to this new field for one or two needed additions to my collection.

# CHAPTER XV.



## A QUICK TRIP THROUGH "THE BUSH."

"THE bush" is the Australian term for the native jungle; and after landing at Melbourne, and admiring the wonderful progress of this comparatively new country and its flourishing capital, we took a fortnight's hard riding to reach it. At the end of that time I found myself installed at the hut of an Australian squatter, on " the run" of a hospitable friend whom I was to visit.

The curious country round us, called, as I have said, "the bush," is a mixture of forest and underbrush, not at all unlike the virgin solitudes of North America or the jungles of India, but without the savage grandeur of the former, or the picturesqueness of the latter, with its interminable network of vines and bamboos, — the haunt of the tiger, the panther, the elephant, and the deadly serpent. But the Australian bush is varied with charming meadows filled with bright flowers and clumps of lofty trees, and this variety extends uninterruptedly as far as your horse can carry you; always the same prairie with its gigantic trees, the same flowers, the same peaceful silence, broken occasionally by the harsh note of a parrot. or the cry of a cockatoo, standing on one foot and lifting his head to watch you pass. Everywhere you are met with cautions not to touch that flower to your lips lest it poison you; not to break that branch lest a tiny thorn may pierce your skin, and you die in convulsions within an hour, and such like cheerful advice. You are surrounded, in fact, with deadly plants, which under a tropic sun distil the most potent poisons; and it is the vegetable, rather than the animal, kingdom that the traveller has to fear.

" The run " had been named by the owner, a friend and countryman of mine, " Devil's Station," because of the savage wildness of the country covered with virgin forests and untracked bush. and he confided to me that he had never himself been entirely round his property. The name was appropriate on account, as well, of this deadly growth of plant life, suggesting to a superstitious mind the magic influence of evil spirits.

The English Government has hit upon the happiest way to colonize this rich country, allowing to the first comer. without regard to " race, color, or previous condition of servitude," the right to take possession of any unoccupied land, — ten, twenty, fifty, or one hundred acres, as much as his resources will allow him to improve to advantage, — demanding in return so small a tax that it simply serves to establish and preserve the royal property in the land. The settler becomes the tenant of the Government, ruling over these vast possessions as he sees fit : the only condition imposed upon him being that he shall receive and entertain for three days any European. wounded. sick, or in want. and supply him with sufficient provision to reach the next station. Any one breaking this rule loses at once all the privileges of his original concession, and, although there are some flagrant abuses resulting from it, as a whole it works well, and has saved many a good fellow's life.

Two days after our arrival our host arranged a kangaroo hunt in our honor, in the native way, — that is, without guns. The night before, a dozen guides were despatched in different directions to scour the country, and report on the prospect of a successful hunt.

At dawn we were awakened by our host, and told to prepare for a day's sport. as the report from the scouts had been favorable. The party consisted of five natives, my host. myself. and Thursday. and three travellers invited at the last moment. One of them brought two enormous dogs in leash, bearing the suggestive names of Strangler and Terror. We were followed by a wagon loaded with provisions and camping conveniences. enough to last us a week, if we chose to stay that long. As the day broke we strangers were all loud in our admiration of the beauty of the landscape. and our words fired the pride of our guides. So we went along well pleased with ourselves and one another.

Here and there, as if dropped pell-mell, without order

AUSTRALIAN KANGAROOS.

or system, our host pointed out all those varieties of giant myrtle and pine, which are unequalled elsewhere in the world; the eucalyptus, — one variety of which is noted for its abundant sap, the growing well of the traveller; and one for its height, often reaching four hundred feet, and rivalling its neighbor, the *Welling-tonia Gigantea*, which grows to even greater heights. Hundreds of varieties of acacia studded the plain, filled in with Australian white lilies of sweetest perfume. We were passing through little clumps of fig-trees, whence a wax-like gum exuded; of *palukas*, bearing a sort of manna; and of silk-trees, whose long green threads swept the ground like hair.

At eleven, or so, we met another of our scouts waiting to advise us of the proximity of the game for which we were in pursuit; and by his advice we left our mustangs under guard of one of the natives, and, rifle in hand, began threading the undergrowth, often so dense and low that we were obliged to advance on hands and knees, stopping every now and then, as the guide listened, his ear near the ground, for any sound of game in the neighborhood. After an hour of this painful advance, the guide told us we had reached the spot where he thought the kangaroos would shortly come; and we lay as he placed us, each behind and, in fact, *in* a bush, so that we could not see one another, so well were we hidden. It was uncomfortable, but necessary. The guide then began the clever imitation of a magpie's note at regular intervals: and even I who knew he was going to do it, and who lay nearest him, half doubted it was not the real article. It was as good as Thursday's imitation of

BY HIS ADVICE WE LEFT OUR MUSTANGS.

the young elephant. Suddenly a light rustling among the leaves drew my eyes in another direction; and there stood a magnificent kangaroo over six feet tall. looking around for the source of the disturbance, which, by the way, ceased instantly.

The light-footed animal approached fearlessly, now stopping and sitting on its haunches to eat a tuft of delicate greens, now dropping on all fours and running forward in a zigzag course as light-heartedly as a child. Soon, reaching the stream, it drank deep draughts from the waters, and, what was our astonishment! out popped from one of its pouches a young one and gambolled on the grass beside its mother. It was a pretty sight, and I, for one, regretted the hostile ambush. But it was too late now to draw off the natives, who could not understand such a motive, and who already held their javelins poised for hurling.

By courtesy, Thursday was allowed the first shot, and, either by luck or a skill which I was ignorant he possessed, his spear was so well aimed that the poor beast fell without a sound, and almost before the fatal steel reached her he ran out, disregarding the cautions of our host to look out for the dying animal's claws, to catch the little one and offer it to me for adoption. I found it old enough to live without its mother, to whom it struggled feebly to return.

Meanwhile the natives had scooped out a hole some two feet deep, and filling it with dead wood and large round pebbles from the river-bed, set fire to the pile, and soon had a pile of red-hot stones and glowing embers. The kangaroo was quickly dressed, and the best parts put into this improvised oven and earthed up for thirty minutes. when they emerged smoking and appetizing. and I must confess I never ate anything better — in Australia!

We passed the night in camp. and the next day returned to our indefatigable mustangs. remounted. and continued our inspection of the run and our search for further adventure. The little kangaroo steadfastly refused all food. and at the end of the second day died of starvation. It was an inglorious ending of a cruel sport. to my mind; and I heartily wished both mother and young alive and free again.

For several days we travelled through the bush. journeying slowly from one enchanted scene to another. — the horses' hoofs sinking into a soft green carpet. stretching far and wide beneath the grateful shade of the gigantic trees; on every side fragrant flowers. yellow, red, purple. and white. arranged as no florist can, and in a profusion unequalled by any forced growth. One of the lilies is periodic in its perfume. as the morning-glory is in bloom. sending out no perfume during the night, but under the magnetic influence of the sun's warmth emitting a most penetrating and agreeable scent. drawing toward it thousands of bees that hang upon its flowers for hours. Another lily. a red variety. *per contra.* seems to languish during the heat of the day. waiting the refreshing dews of evening to open. When twilight comes it arouses from its lethargy. holds up its beautiful

IT STRUGGLED TO ESCAPE FROM MY HANDS.

head, and pours a flood of fragrant incense into the night, closing again at early dawn.

The silence of the prairies oppressed us, for not a bird's note disturbs these solitudes; although later we found that there *were* plenty of winged beauties on the continent — but of that and the odd way in which we became convinced of it, later.

We saw many kangaroos, but without harming them; even the natives seeming to have been touched by the death of our little captive. They are timid, graceful animals, of great variety of size, and should only be killed when their excellent meat is needed.

I passed my days adding to my herbarium and collection of insects, and my rifle hung, a useless ornament, at my saddle-bow. One of these peaceful mornings, I was riding along with my party, when I noticed occasional glances of alarm cast over his shoulder by our leading bushman. The day had opened clear and bright, when, suddenly and without warning, the wind began to rise and blow in a most threatening way through the trees, bending their lofty trunks, and tearing the leaves from the branches. I was old enough woodsman to understand why the Australians looked anxious and turned their horses toward the denser forest, where the trees would shelter us from the approaching cyclone. Great black clouds scurried across the sky, and showed us we must hurry to reach any shelter before the storm should break.

"We still have a few minutes' lee-way," said our host.

"for a cyclone is always preceded by a flight of birds escaping from it. — just as we are, but with better success."
Almost as he spoke the sound of innumerable wings was

I WAS URGING ON MY NAG WITH SPUR AND VOICE.

heard, and a dense flight of birds passed over our heads, uttering their discordant cries, as if defying the gale behind them.

I was urging on my plucky nag with spur and voice, and she seemed to understand the necessity of effort, " devouring the ground " beneath her flying feet, while overhead the forked lightning lit up the inky sky. It was an impressive sight, its very suddenness adding to its grandeur. I must have resembled the phantom rider of the Norwegian ballads, who only appears on days when kings or great men die : tearing across the country flat upon his fiery steed, with the black clouds of misfortune and death behind him. Like a cannon-ball the cyclone struck us, and carried my stout mare forward as irresistibly as if she had been a feather. It was impossible to stop or to turn aside. Forward! was the only word ; and the fact that a tiny lake lay directly in front of us made no difference whatever to the wind god, and into the water we went, horse and man, in obedience to his mighty breath. This seemed to pacify him instantly, or else he had done his worst, for the wind fell as promptly as it had arisen, leaving me to haul myself out by an overhanging branch, none the worse for my bath, while the poor pony waded ashore at the nearest beach : and together we sought our companions, scattered far and wide, like dead leaves before the blast. No one had been hurt ; and we were congratulating ourselves upon the escape of the party all through our lunch hour, which we prolonged to several, resting our tired horses and excited guides, who whiled away the time telling stories of less fortunate parties, overtaken by these sudden tropical gales, and never heard from afterward. Just as we were starting on once more, our chief guide interrupted our chat and laughter by laying his finger on his lips, and pointing toward a tall eucalyptus near which we had been lunching.

" What is it, Nagarnook ?" queried our host.

The guide moved silently round the tree, his hands clasped negligently behind his back, scrutinizing with his bead-like eyes every point of its polished bark. After a moment or two of this examination, he stopped and uttered one word : " Opossum ! "

" How, in the name of all that 's good, does he know ? " laughed I.

A smile of conscious pride passed over the face of the native. who understood my tone of surprise, as with his finger he pointed out to me a line of tiny scratches, hardly visible, in the smooth bark of the giant tree.

" Yes, but they may be old marks. What makes you believe them recent ? "

" The white chief is pleased to jest with his slave."

" No. seriously : I see that they are opossum marks, but the trees are full of just such tracks all around us."

" Let the white chief look more closely ; " and he showed me in the marks lowest down on the trunk, grains of sand. damp still, and evidently recently left behind a climbing 'possum. Blowing hard upon these the sand still clung to the moistened track. He looked up. proud of his proof.

WE PROLONGED OUR LUNCH HOUR.

"Well done!  But how can we get at him?  Let us see you solve that difficulty!"

Without waiting to be asked twice, Nagarnook seized his hatchet and cut a foothold in the base of the tree a yard up, and another a yard above that.  Placing his toes in this improvised ladder, and with his left arm embracing the mighty trunk, he lifted himself, and with his right cut a new rest higher up, and so on until he reached the lower branches, where the animal's hole was.  Into this he ran his hand, and seizing the fellow by his tail to avoid his sharp teeth, he swung him round his head several times, and brained him on his own doorstep, and then dropped him at our feet in triumph.  It was all so neatly and quickly done, that we could not help a shout of applause, as he descended in the same way he had gone up.

The little animal was cooked for supper; and it was now so late, we decided to camp where we were.  The meat of the 'possum—which is about three times as large as a gray squirrel—is bitter and detestable to a European palate; but the native guides thought it delicious, and made a perfect feast of it.

The night was enlivened by the cry with which this animal salutes its coming, and which it utters as it seeks its food from branch to branch in the darkness.  This note was like a bugle-call to the natives, who quickly lighted pine torches, and started in pursuit with their boomerangs as arms, and bagged over a dozen before they were satisfied to turn in for the night.

The boomerang is an arm purely Australian in invention and use, and I have never seen it carried in any other country on the globe. It varies in length from two feet and a half to three feet, and is fashioned from a hard though flexible bit of wood, slightly curved in the middle, rounded at one end, and quite flat at the other. It is not so wholly unlike a Yankee axe-handle in shape, though in color it is almost always as much darker as the color of Australian woods is deeper than those of New England.

When the native wishes to use his boomerang, he seizes it at the larger end in both hands, the convex side up, then whirling it rapidly round his head with a peculiar motion of the wrist, that gives it its terrible force and accuracy of return, he lets it go into the air. Thus hurled it travels some dozen yards, which is simply preliminary. At the instant it touches the ground it rebounds several feet, and returns upon its track until it reaches the object against which its thrower intended it to strike.

They tell a curious story of this weapon, so deadly in an Australian's hands. When one of the first explorers returned to England, and told of its marvellous accuracy and execution, the learned doctors at Oxford laughed at him, and one in particular took especial delight in pointing out the physical impossibility of such feats, and sneering at the narrator. A few months afterward this disbeliever was sent by his confrères to Australia on some

HE SWUNG HIM ROUND HIS HEAD SEVERAL TIMES.

mission connected with his profession, and had occasion to prove the truth of the story he had doubted.

Placed face to face with a native chief, he asked the latter to exhibit his skill with the boomerang, taking him as his mark; and, folding his arms, he stood smilingly awaiting the result. The chief, although somewhat surprised, asked nothing better, and, with a hasty glance at the professor, hurled his weapon into the air. After describing several graceful curves, it came back swiftly toward its mark whistling viciously, and it would certainly have broken the doctor's sceptical skull, had he not prudently thrown himself flat on the ground in a paroxysm of terror, from which he emerged in a wiser, if not a happier, frame of mind.

We should have been glad to stop this unnecessary slaughter of opossums; but, as our host said, you could no more convince the natives of the cruelty they were needlessly inflicting, than you could induce them to alter their religion in favor of one in which transmigration should play a part. A sudden end was put to the *sport*, however, in an unlooked-for way, by the cries of terror and pain which one of the natives uttered at this moment. We did not understand the language, but we caught the feeling vividly; and the whole camp rushed toward the sufferer, rolling in agony beside the stream, his head apparently wrapped in a black turban.

"What's the matter with him?" shouted one of our party. Without waiting to reply, the chief guide drew his knife. and quick as thought laid the black band open its entire length. revealing the tortured features and wounded forehead of his countryman beneath. For it was one of the terrible reptiles of the country that had fallen. like a leech. upon the poor fellow, and was slowly sucking away his life-blood. As it dropped off we saw six large wounds. from which the blood flowed freely. on the guide's face, and a real bandage was immediately applied. and such prompt remedies administered as experience had taught: for delay is death. After this accident naturally enough the hunt was brought to a sudden end. and we turned our horses seaward. our journey enlivened by stories of this frightful scourge, which. fortunately. is as rare as it is terrible: indeed, my host said that in twenty years of knocking round the bush. this was but the third he had seen. And my tempting offer of a year's supply of rum and tobacco to any native who would bring me a specimen alive. failed to produce one within the next two weeks, during which I remained in the country.

The next morning as we were preparing to mount, one of the men called our attention to a swarm of bees, and a very large one. on a branch of mimosa. their legs covered with the rich pollen. and apparently quite forgetful of their hive. Each native immediately set to work making himself a tiny cage from reeds: and into this, with marvellous skill. and the aid of some bit of bloom particularly appetizing to these

QUICK AS THOUGHT HE DREW HIS KNIFE.

"friends of flowers," as they are poetically called there. each tempted a few bees, and shut them in safely. None of the white men interfered in this dangerous

LEAVING HIM, LIKE MAZEPPA, AT THE BEAST'S MERCY.

operation, nor did we understand its object, but watched with admiration while they handled these peppery little fellows without a sting.

When each had captured about a dozen, the chief

explained to our host how they proposed by these prisoners to discover the hive, and obtain a coveted supply of honey.

In five minutes we were all in the saddle, and, the Australians leading, started in the direction in which the first bee, when liberated, flew. As soon as we were distanced by this rapid guide. another was let go, and so on, until, at the tremendous pace we were going, I felt we must have travelled twenty miles, for we did not even draw rein when a fresh bee was freed. The pace was beginning to tell on one of our party, and afterward he confessed to me he had never ridden so hard in his life. To add to his sufferings, his saddle began to slip, and, cling as he might, it surely and slowly disappeared beneath his horse's belly, leaving him. like Mazeppa. at the beast's mercy. It was no laughing matter. although he did appear most supremely ridiculous; for. riding as hard as we could, we could not catch his frightened pony, which easily led the hunt. Luckily for him, the animal entered into the pursuit with intelligence as well as zest; and when at last the dead tree. groaning beneath its weight of stored sweets, was reached, he stopped with the rest, and ended his mad career as gently as he had begun it.

Loaded with honey, we continued our way at a more comfortable jog, reaching our host's broad verandas in time to enjoy a more luxurious bed than we had seen for many nights.

Before bidding farewell to my hospitable friend and Thursday, — whom I bequeathed to him, when I found the latter was willing, — I made one brief hunting trip

I FOUND SEVERAL SMALL FISH IN HIS STOMACH.

in another direction, which introduced me to a curious bat-like animal, with a description of which I may most appropriately close this wandering narrative, which perhaps resembles it, — half-bird and half-mammal.

I had shot a couple of foxes, and was "toting" them into camp, when I heard a rustling in the underbrush along a stream running beside the trail, and out hopped a frog-like bat, with the tail of a beaver! This is the best way I can describe him, even after shooting and dissecting him. He was like an American beaver in other respects than his broad. flat tail; but his throat and long web-footed hind legs were those of a frog; while the membrane from his fore-feet to his side resembled the wings of a bat.

Opening this curiosity carefully, I found several small fish in his stomach. and an old button! — certainly a light breakfast! I took the greatest pains with this specimen, wishing to identify it when I returned to America, and packed it with my most valued possessions. intrusting the package to Thursday, who insisted on going back to Melbourne to see me safely off. But I was fated never to see it again. Between the wharf, where I parted with the faithful fellow, and the hold of the vessel the package mysteriously disappeared; and I have never been quite sure whether I was the victim of a practical joke. or whether I really was the discoverer of a new species. of which the knowledge perished with the lost package.

University Press: John Wilson and Son, Cambridge

9 783337 045791